The Teenage Diary

Everything I Never Planned

Pehal Bhandari

AF651797

BlueRose ONE.com
Stories Matter
NewDelhi • London

BLUEROSE PUBLISHERS
India | U.K.

Copyright © Pehal Bhandari 2025

All rights reserved by author. No part of this publication may be reproduced, stored in a retrieval system or transmitted in any form or by any means, electronic, mechanical, photocopying, recording or otherwise, without the prior permission of the author. Although every precaution has been taken to verify the accuracy of the information contained herein, the publisher assumes no responsibility for any errors or omissions. No liability is assumed for damages that may result from the use of information contained within.

BlueRose Publishers takes no responsibility for any damages, losses, or liabilities that may arise from the use or misuse of the information, products, or services provided in this publication.

BlueRose ONE.com
Stories Matter
NewDelhi • London

For permissions requests or inquiries regarding this publication, please contact:

BLUEROSE PUBLISHERS
www.BlueRoseONE.com
info@bluerosepublishers.com
+91 8882 898 898
+4407342408967

ISBN: 978-93-7310-117-0

Cover design: Yash Singhal
Typesetting: Namrata Saini

First Edition: October 2025

Dedication

For my parents, who stood by me through every mood, mistake, and meltdown. This book began as their idea, but it became my memory.

Preface

This book started as nothing more than scribbles in the margins of classes I never really paid attention to. It was messy, imperfect, just me — raw, restless, honest. And maybe that's the whole point of *The Teenage Diary*. It was never meant to be polished like Instagram highlights or wrapped up neatly in filters. It was meant to be real, a place where I could trap my teenage years before they slipped away into the black hole of memory.

I wrote this book so that when I grow up, when life feels too heavy, too suffocating, too "mature" for its own good, I can come back here. I can flip through these pages and remind myself that pain doesn't last forever — that life might be bad for a short time, but it can also be breathtakingly good for a very long time. It all depends on how you choose to live it.

People post their teenage years on Snapchat stories or Instagram reels, but I wanted mine here — someplace safer, someplace still. A record that even in my future, I can hand to the people around me and say, *This is how much I have lived, even before I fully knew how much I was supposed.* I've always followed my heart, without even realizing it.

I've never always been surrounded by good people. I've been too sweet, too kind in the eyes of my family, and at the same time,there were times when, I've been seen unfiltered, and ugly by my friends. And the truth? I've not always been the "good person" either. I've had my bad moments, my reckless phases, my puberty hitting me in ways I never expected. I've been selfish, messy, dramatic, and sometimes downright unlikeable. But all through it I've always been real.

Writing this teenage diary has made me fearless of the fact that, *What if people read it?* So what if they do? It's my story. My mess. My voice. I get to shape it.

I cried for the most unrealistic little things — and somehow those tiny, stupid tears changed my perspective more than the "big" milestones ever could. I used to believe only big changes mattered: the CEO dreams, the IIT obsession. I told myself I'd run the world, but I ended up choosing the arts, a stream that lets me express myself instead of confining me. I was once fascinated by IIT's e-summits and MUNs, but, now I'm fascinated by the idea of brands, identity, and voice. I changed, and I love the change.

And yet, I'm terrified of being trapped in things that don't feel real. Nude beaches don't scare me. What scares me is a life that feels fake, suffocating, too traditional. Because I know I can be bare even without clothes. Realness has always mattered more to me than rules. I love change. I live for it. But at the same time, I ache for constants. I want time to stop and move at the same time. I want to explore, but I don't want to let go of what's here. I'm nostalgic like that — constantly crying over people who don't care about me, and crying harder for the ones who do.

I've been told I have "too much of an attitude." Maybe I did. Maybe I didn't. Back then, when I said I didn't care about people's opinions, the truth is I cared too much. Now? I actually don't. That's growth. That's why I can write this book, unbothered, carefree.

This isn't just storytelling. This is me documenting my past, while secretly rewriting my future. This is me admitting I'm not scared of failure — I'm scared of becoming the background noise. Because the unforgettable people in my life were never the ones who clung to their biggest, most dramatic stories. They were the ones who kept creating new ones, without begging the world to notice.

I want to be like that. That's what this book is. These chapters are my stories, my old highlight reels, which keep nudging me to create new ones. To keep living with the same intensity as I write. To never shrink. To never let life feel small.

Maybe you're my future self holding this book years later, maybe you're a stranger who picked it up out of curiosity, or maybe you're another teenager trying to survive your own storm. Whoever you are, I hope you see yourself in these pages — not in the polished parts, but in the clutter, the contradictions, the tiny victories that felt like revolutions.

It matters because people dismiss teenage years as "just a phase," as if our tears and rebellions don't count. But I know they do. The nights I cried myself to sleep, the mornings I fought with my mom over nothing and everything, the times I was wrong and the times I didn't even care — they weren't small. They shaped me. And they deserve to be remembered, not brushed aside.

So here it is — messy, brutal, funny, nostalgic, insecure, confident, loving, selfish, brave, scared — all of it. My teenage diary. My way of reminding myself that every moment, good or bad, deserves to be remembered.

Letter to My Future Self

I hope you're living the life we always dreamed of—dancing on the beaches of Europe, chasing sunsets in Miami, swaying under neon lights of Finland, and risking your life just to live, laugh and love. I hope you're working in places you once whispered about to yourself, places so bold that they felt like daydreams—, Or maybe you've built something entirely on your own, a brand with your name on it, a name people speak with admiration, not just for your work, but for the force of your presence.

I hope you're not only admired but remembered—by children you've lifted in faraway villages, by women you've helped stand taller, by the voices you've amplified even when yours was shaking. I hope you're reckless with kindness, generous to the point where ninety percent of your income feels like it belongs to the world anyway. And yet, I hope you don't forget to spend on yourself too—on luxury, on beauty, on experiences that remind you that money is meant to be lived with, not hoarded. Don't only dream to become a CEO, you can even be the member of UNICEF.

I hope you've carried your mother across countries, put the world in her hands the way she once put crayons in yours. I hope you've tried everything that once made you tremble—singing too loudly, standing too boldly, wearing what you weren't "supposed to", even living a 9-to-5 job just so, to prove to yourself why you hated it. Life is not survival, it's trial, and you were never born to tiptoe.

I hope you've loved and lost and loved again. Maybe your first love stayed, maybe he didn't, but I hope you always honored the truth of what he meant to you. I hope you found the courage to marry the first person who deserved the whole of you—or the courage to walk away if he didn't. And if you've had your breaks, your mistakes, your reckless moments in Italy, France, or London—laugh about them. You were made to be remembered, not erased.

I hope you don't just collect friends, but build a tribe of strangers who became family in coffee shops, airports, messy college nights. And I hope you don't forget the family who raised you either—the ones whose love is not aesthetic but real, and sometimes even suffocating. Don't let your success make you distant. The people who fought with you, who hurt you, who made you cry—they were also the ones who shaped your fire. Remember them, always.

I hope you've stood on a stage and made people laugh until their ribs hurt, even if your own ribs ached from a fight the night before. I hope you've spoken for those who couldn't, written for those who were silenced, turned your worst memories into stories that made someone else feel less alone.

But more than all that—I hope you've stayed kind. Not soft, not naïve, but kind. Because you never know what battles the person across you is fighting, and you were always the girl who believed in lighting candles in the dark, even when your own hands shook holding the match.

And future me—don't forget me. The teenage you. The girl who's writing this with swollen eyes, messy hair, and too many dreams for a single lifetime. The girl who was dramatic enough to plan naked beach runs and tender enough to cry over the sound of rain. Don't bury her beneath success. She's the reason you exist. Carry her along.

Above all, I hope you built a life you don't just live, but a life you can laugh about, cry about, brag about, regret about—and still, at the end of the day, whisper, *"Yes, this was mine."*

And to you, my future self — no matter where you are, whatever position you've landed in, whatever choices you've made, I am already so impossibly proud of you. Proud not because of the brands you worked for, or the stamps on your passport, or the applause you collected, but because you survived the girl I am today. You carried her fears — the nights of grade 11 when the world felt too heavy, the grade 12 doubts that kept her staring at the ceiling — and you still became someone. You did not let her drown. You taught her that strength isn't loud, it's in showing up even when your chest is caving in.

And listen — don't think strength means never crying. Cry when it's too much. Cry even if it feels unworthy, even if someone says it isn't "big enough" to break you. Cry over the little humiliations, the unfair grades, the moments when love feels one-sided, the days when your body aches with exhaustion. Cry, and then stand up again. Just don't let your tears ever convince you that you are weak. Because you never were, and you never will be.

"Kindergarten taught me that even the smallest heartbreaks can feel like the end of the world."

Contents

Chapter 1

Kindergarten Tears and Untied Shoelaces

Dear Diary,

I don't remember the details. But I remember the feelings.

I remember sitting outside the bathroom door, waiting for Dada to finish brushing, just so, talking to him would be the first thing in the morning. He always made time for me — always. More than anyone else ever did. My world didn't begin with school, it began with Dada's lap and Dadi's stories. And strangely, even now, that feels more real than anything that came after.

My parents were... there. Of course. But I was never their girl. I was *theirs* — my grandparents'. My Dadi would braid my hair with such patience, and my Dada would bring home books — *real books* — for a baby who couldn't even walk or talk properly. "Apple", "Mango", "Banana", he'd say. "Say it with me". And I did. I don't remember my first steps, but I remember that.

Everyone says first-borns are always spoiled. But I wasn't spoiled. I was celebrated.

My first birthday? A new cycle. Family from everywhere came over — like it was a festival. Not because I was special. But because I was their first, but luckily I never had the "eldest daughter should grow too fast-thing" myth, in my family, even after the upbringing of my younger siblings, I was never had that pressure, to win, to mature at the age of 9, it was always me who wanted to be ahead, but ended up being a kid at 17, I guess that's what my people always wanted, to enjoy, to laugh, to let them still bribe me with silly 10 rupee chocolates. It all started before I could even pronounce my name.

I was a Kidzee kid. Uniform too big. Hair always messed. Shoes never tied. I had this rickshaw — Laksh Auto — that came every day. I hated it and loved it. It took me away from home but also took me to the stage.

That stage.

Where I won my first dance competition.

Where I made my first sandwich — as a chef in some kids' food fest.

Where I held my first trophy for "Best Student."

I didn't even know what that meant. I just knew it made everyone clap. And I liked that sound. Applause. Maybe that's why I chase it even now.

But it wasn't always applause. Some mornings, I cried before school. Sometimes quietly. Sometimes not. The smell of my uniform, the sound of my shoelaces dragging, the feeling of being too small for the big world — it overwhelmed me.

But I went.

And I smiled.

And I danced.

And I made my mother shape balloons into heart goals and told her, *"I scored!"* when I kicked an imaginary ball through it.

I had teachers who loved me. I had classmates who followed me around. And I had stories I didn't know I was writing, even back then. I had friends who I used to bully, I remember being dragged to boys washroom in senior kg, by my idiot guy friends, and the first time being scolded by my principal for it, I remember breaking one of the guy friend's shinchan watch that he got for his birthday , and crying to play that innocent girly charm. Funny how he was the same guy I played kitchen set, makeup set, fort buildings and other boyish kinda girly with stuff.

Sometimes I think I peaked too early. Other times, I think I just started early. Maybe both are true. All I know is, even back then, I felt everything too deeply.

When I was four, life gave me my brother. I don't remember every detail, but I know it was the best gift I could have ever received. He wasn't my age, not someone to played dolls and go to school with, but he became my partner in gossip during family functions, the one I could roll my eyes at when relatives started their boring speeches. Brotherhood, in its purest, simplest form.

Even when it was just crayons and storybooks and skipping rhymes...

I already had a whole world inside me.

And no one noticed how much I was carrying.

They just saw my gold star.

I was a good kid.

A quiet storm.

A not so soft voice in the backseat of Laksh Auto, holding trophies, still wiping tears but,

Memories are messy and somehow, they have always asked to be written twice: once in truth, once in the feelings. So here's the feeling part…

I learned that even the smallest appreciations could make someone feel the happiest in the world. That a tiny gift could change your entire day, your entire perspective. That we were so small, so unaware, so unprepared to understand anything at all—but somehow, even in our little world, these tiny moments mattered more than we could ever know.

Too young to be loud.

In a house where love smelled like cardamom tea,
I was not just a daughter — I was royalty.
Dada's shadow followed me through every hour,
He waited at doors like a sun-kissed flower.
He'd hum old songs outside the bathroom door,
While I counted tiles on the cold mosaic floor.
He was magic wrapped in a cotton kurta,
And I? His chosen sidekick in every saga.
Before school bells rang and benches aligned,
Life was Laksh Rickshaw, bumpy yet kind.
Tiny fingers waving at passing trees,
Kidzee bags and scraped-up knees.
One day I danced like the world stood still,
Another, I cooked — bread, butter, thrill.
A sandwich made with clumsy pride,
Mom said, "Chef of the Year!" — I didn't hide.
I wore balloons once as a costume crown,
A shy princess in a paper gown.
And when they called my name on stage,
The trophy glittered brighter than my age.
Shoelaces tangled, tears like pearls,
Still, I was braver than most of the girls.
They cheered, "Best student!" — I didn't even know
That gold stars would come and quietly go.

I didn't know life gets harder than glue,
That friends grow apart and medals fade too.
But in that world of crayons and cheers,
I lived — wildly, softly — my kindergarten years.

Chapter 2

Sticky Notes and Class Monitor Badges

(Dear Diary... this one's for the long-lost chaos of primary school)

Dear Diary,

SGIS. I still don't know how to say that school's name without either laughing or rolling my eyes. I mean, Sanjay Ghodawat International School? Sounds fancy, right? Like one of those polished schools where kids are supposed to walk in a straight line and say "Good morning, ma'am" in perfect unison. But for me? It was a little bit of everything — terrifying at first, hilarious in between, and eventually? Just... mine. And when I turned six, my sister came along—my aunt's daughter, my 4 a.m. person, my clothes-sharing partner, my mirror in so many ways. I look at her now and can't believe how much she has grown. She's still so small, but she has become this permanent part of my story, stitched into the mess and magic of my childhood.

Those two weren't just people added to my life. They were the greatest gifts my family could ever give me. Like I remember teaching them dance. Making them sneak out in the tent house I had in my (our) room. I was a good elder sister unknowingly at that time I guess. I had it all—my kingdom of childhood. The biggest kitchen set you could imagine, two makeup kits (one surprise from my mom, because she knew me too well), a doctor set, and even a tent house. My friends—boys and girls alike—used to come over and play kitchen with me, doctor with me, set up camp in my little tent. One side of my room was a bustling mini home, oven, fruits to cut, salt shakers, tiny hangers—everything in its place, everything alive. The other side? Makeup galore, brushes and powders everywhere. I lived the peak of girly heaven, and I adored every second of it. That room wasn't just toys; it was me, in all my girly glory.

Now coming to the school and everything, the worst part? I didn't even want to go there. When I first heard the name, I genuinely thought it sounded like some "ghoda-ghoda" school. Don't judge. I was little, okay? But obviously, I went. And like most things I didn't want — it ended up becoming something I'd never forget.

I was the kid with the neat notes. The one who *actually* updated her notebooks after holidays. Like, who even does that? But I was proud of it. Still am, if I'm being honest. I liked being that girl. The one teachers trusted with to keep things in order when they left the class. The one who got the "best handwriting" star. The one with the straight back and the badge on the chest and that whole "responsible" vibe. But also... the same girl who once hit a boy with his own skates. Yep. Real story. He hit me back with a writing board, so don't worry — we're even. I was always naughty since childhood, but I loved the attention more than the flies in my stomach. And yes I couldn't hold them any longer, so they skipped, thus I chose to be both, till….

I remember once, someone told me that if you sucked ink refills from the back, the ink would last longer. I believed them. Because obviously, I was a genius. So there I was — third grade Pehal — sucking a neon pink pen refill like a straw. Next thing I knew, I had a mouth full of ink and a lifetime supply of shame. I ran to the washroom with my tongue stained pink and my brain screaming "*what the hell did I just do?*" I didn't even like science, and yet there I was — being my own stupid experiment.

We had this rule — or maybe it was just a random thing that became a rule — that the first one in line got to hold the teacher's hand while going to the bus bay. Everyone used to race to the front. I was that kid. *That* was the ultimate privilege. But weirdly, somewhere around fifth grade, it flipped. Suddenly, everyone wanted to be the last. Maybe we just wanted to grow up. Maybe holding ma'am's hand wasn't cool anymore. Maybe the back of the line felt more... like a place we should dance.

Primary school had its own version of drama. There was this time in third when my girls literally pushed me towards a guy — like shoved me, physically — and I ended up screaming in his ear. Not a cute squeal. No. A full-blown horror movie scream. He looked like I'd electrocuted him. I wanted the ground to eat me alive. They laughed for days.

My friendships in primary school were weirdly lopsided. I always *wanted* to be closer to the girls. I did have some, and they were lovely. But somehow, I always ended up closer to the boys — not in that *flirty* way, just in a "we understand each other better" way. I wanted deep female friendships, I craved them. But until seventh grade, it was mostly guy friends I hung out with. They were easier, less complicated — or maybe I just didn't know how to handle all the layers that came with girlhood back then.

I even got into a salsa partner war with one of my close girlfriends. I didn't even *like* the boy — she did. And somehow, just us being paired with him became a whole cold war. I didn't know what I did wrong. I just remember feeling confused and sad and awkward. Like, am I a villain or am I just existing?

But amid the mess, there were safe spaces.

God, Asha Ma'am. If there's ever been a teacher who understood me — actually *understood* me — it was her. She was the one I'd cry to when things got too much. And she never once made me feel like I was too sensitive or too dramatic or too much. She just... listened. Loved. Held space. And I held on to her, tightly. The best part she was my class teacher in grade 1 and still after all these years, nothing's changed.

I also had my *dada*. Every single day, without fail, he'd be at the bus stop waiting for me. And almost every time, he had a chocolate. I still remember those wrappers crinkling in my sweaty little palm. I think that's where I first felt what unconditional love feels like. Just showing up. No matter what. As much as I was innocent in front of dada, my mom was done with me after this one incident where I cut my hair down to those silly little cute bangs, that made me look like a potato or worse, tried hiding it but ended up getting slapped right across my face.

Also, we had this epic school trip to the chairman's farmhouse. I was pissed about being put in a different section that year — none of my close friends were there. I thought it would ruin everything. But the trip? It was amazing. One of those weird lessons from the universe: you don't always get what you want, but what you get sometimes turns out better. This trip made me realize that not being put in a different section was the best thing that happened that year. I got my best friend, I got to be the leader, the glue of the class, those gathering practices, movie sessions, gossiping at 10, crying for a lost pencil, the untitled crew, the real boy girl drama cheat, tripping each other off but at the same time holding each others hand, laughing, bunking, playing bad, and curating things of our own in the science lab was where we realized.. this is our last primary year and so far the best .

There was inter-house football too. I was never sporty, like not the girl you'd expect to run across a field and tackle someone for a ball. But no one from my house signed up, so guess who got dragged in? Me. I was mad about it, didn't want to play. But then we won. And that feeling — that we're-in-this-together rush? Yeah, I kinda loved it. I guess that's where I realized my love for football, Ronaldo and Europe.

I even remember this one boy — poor guy — he had a body odour problem, and the whole class used to tease him. Even me. Looking back, it wasn't fair. It wasn't kind. I've outgrown it now, I swear. But childhood isn't always innocent. Sometimes it's stupid, sometimes it's mean, and sometimes it teaches you who you never want to become again.

SGIS was that weird mix of glitter and mess. Of gold stars and fights. Of poetry recitals and refill ink disasters. Of shifting sections and emotional overreactions. It was sticky notes and class monitor badges, crying in sick rooms and laughing five minutes later. It was the chaos I didn't plan but somehow always belonged to. And maybe, just maybe, it was the first place I started becoming *me* — messy, mouthy, emotional, responsible, chaotic me.

Also you know, my mother made me sleep at 8 p.m, as soon as it dawned, she used to keep me an all-oily-headed person, 2 braids, knee length socks, and I listened to her, because for me she was and still is the only sensible person, who my family claims to be strict, but no, she is the coolest person alive, (keeping her anger aside).

It was too early for me to read life the way it really was, but even in those primary years, I picked up something. I learned that being the "naughtiest" kid in the room isn't always cool—it's just noisy. I realized the things that glitter from the outside are not always the same on the inside. Half the time, we overthink, assume, twist people's words and stares in our heads, and then regret it later. But sometimes, the decisions you make in that exact mess—the ones you didn't polish or rehearse—turn out to be the best ones of your life. So, here's the truth I carry: be clumsy, be naughty, be chaotic if that's who you are. Just don't be fake. Be real. Be real with yourself first, and then with the world. Because there's nothing braver than letting people see you unfiltered.

Even when I wasn't that young, I realized something amazing about myself—I was leaking memories, but I didn't care about who was coming or going, who was drifting away. I was just focused on myself. That unbothered, unapologetic version of me… it's something I should probably try to channel even now. I was present, yet thriving, surrounded by people, yet untethered.

It also taught me that trying something new might just uncover a favorite hobby, or a favorite teacher might make a subject your passion. It showed me that experiences you resist or people you think you can't stand—sometimes end up shaping you in ways you never expected. And now? I want to be that unbothered self again, but the truth is… I'm attached.

Silent Whispers

I was the girl with the neatest notes,
The one teachers praised like a gold-star quote.
Class monitor badge stabbed proud on my shirt,
But inside, I still chased the hurt—
Wanting friends I never quite got to convert.
In fifth, I hit a boy with his own skates,
He hit back with a writing board — perfect mates.
We got scolded, laughed outside the sick room gates,
That's how we said sorry, through laughter and fights,
Not apologies or clean-slate rites.
I changed classes for friends who didn't stay,
Played football because no one else would that day.
Ended up winning and cheering anyway,
That's how life showed me: chaos turns gold,
When you just stop planning how stories unfold.
One of the Ma'am's became my safe little shrine,
When everything cracked, I'd run to her line.
Tears, hugs, and poems in her English time—
She wasn't just a teacher, she was calm in my storm,
A second parent in strict school uniform.
Some days I wanted to be first in the line,
To hold the teacher's hand and pretend it was mine.
Then we grew up and that wasn't the sign—
The cool ones were last, messing around,
Laughing in corners, barely bus-bound.
I blew through a refill, ink spilled in my mouth,
Pink neon shame, tasted worse than south.

I wanted to disappear, but I laughed it out loud,
Because that's who I was— a mix of pride and mess,
Half topper, half chaos in a schoolgirl's dress.
Dada brought me chocolates every morning, slow,
The softest gesture before I had to grow.
Sweetness unwrapped in school-time flow,
And maybe no one noticed that kind of love—
But I kept every wrapper like they were notes from above

Chapter 3

The Girl Who Ate Marks Like Candy

Dear diary,

I don't know what exactly it was — hunger, pride, addiction — but I used to eat marks like candy.

Seriously. Like I wasn't learning algebra or nouns or the state capitals of India — I was collecting scores. Rushing through MCQs just to get the full 10/10, and then staring at the teacher's face until she said it out loud in front of everyone. I wanted to be the girl whose name stuck like highlighter ink on the top of every test paper. The one who didn't just top the class, but did it again and again, like a magic trick no one else could learn.

And you know what? I *was* her. For a long time.

It was this weird, glittery phase of my life where marks tasted better than actual candy. Better than Dairy Milk Silk. Better than the English waffle I used to crave after school. Because every time I aced something, rewards came pouring in like it was Diwali. My dad once promised me, "If you get Rank 1 in Grade 3 finals, I'll get you an iPad." And of course I did. Not because of the iPad (okay, a little because of it), but because that thrill of achieving something — that look of pride on my family's face — it just made me feel like I was meant to shine.

He bought me that iPad in Grade 6, and guess what? I *still* have it. It's ancient now, still runs smoothly, and I wish to never throw it away. It's more than a screen — it's a trophy, a memory. A proof that I could be brilliant when I really want to be.

But then came the fall.

I don't know how to explain it, but somewhere between the pressure and the pandemic, I stopped tasting the candy. It just didn't hit anymore. In online classes, I became this sneaky, sleepy version of myself. I wasn't solving, I was googling. I wasn't asking doubts, I was muting the call. My notes turned into screenshots. My study routine became binge-watching YouTube, skipping math homework, and watching Harry Potter like it was a religion. I'd sit in class with the camera off, half-listening, half-daydreaming. And the worst part? I didn't even feel guilty. Not until it started showing up in my scores — slowly, then all at once.

There was this time in Grade 6 when I got full marks in Math — a full 50/50 — and people literally went after me like I had committed a crime. "She doesn't deserve it," some whispered. "No one gets full in Math." My marks got reduced *because of jealousy.* I mean, what kind of twisted system punishes you for being good?

Then I had this frenemy — . We were both toppers, both secretly annoyed by each other. We never said it, but it was obvious — silent rivalry in every test. But by Grade 8, we became best friends. Isn't that funny? How someone you compete with for years can become someone you'd copy from in tuitions later?

Copying, oh god, let's talk about that. Grade 7 and 8 were literally the Copycat Years. Half syllabus me, half syllabus her — we'd exchange answers mid-exam like it was a business deal. Teachers knew. Some even chased us around class like it was a comedy show. But I didn't care. My brain was tired, and my heart was lonelier than it had ever been. All I wanted was to pass, to breathe, to feel like I wasn't drowning.

But then came Grade 9 — and no, I won't say "I came back stronger" like in some dramatic movie scene. But yeah, something did shift. I joined this new tuition — but the vibe? It clicked. My tutor actually *saw* me. She told me she was proud that I was doing sports, extracurriculars *and* scoring well. She noticed things others missed. She called out the better version of me. She reminded me that I didn't have to be the girl who copied anymore but yet this year I copied the most out of it, with that who sat just behind me, we were in the same tuition too, we really clicked it through, the entire class called that cheating in exams duo, as we split those chapters for exams, never realized when those silly things turned us down to speak about darkest secrets, cycle rides, chips and dirty friendly talks.

I don't know what got into me that day. It was Grade 2, science exam, and I was almost done with my paper — but I kept looking around to see how many kids had finished. And then my eyes fell on his paper — my friend, whose roll number was just behind mine. He'd drawn the most *gorgeous* umbrella. Like, I can still picture it — colorful, neat, artistic. It made mine look like a sad potato. So I did what any irrational, overly expressive, umbrella-loving seven-year-old would do: I asked if we could switch papers so he could draw it on mine too. And he *agreed.* And then... we got caught. By the *vice principal*. It was terrifying and so stupidly funny. I mean, for a damn umbrella? But also... I kind of get her. That tiny me. She just wanted something beautiful on her paper. We were such little idiots. But also, what a memory.

I had a friend too — . A bench partner who laughed when I laughed, stayed when I cried. No drama, no competition — just warmth. The kind of friend who reminded me that school wasn't just a jungle of ranks and percentages. It could also be a place of healing.

And oh, Grade 10.

People say it's a myth —that "it's the best year of school" — but it's *not*. It's real. Grade 10 is chaos and calm, heartbreak and hugging your best friend before the board exam, craving Maggi at 10 PM, and somehow still pulling off 94.6% with average-at-best preparation. I barely studied — not because I didn't care, but because I *cared* too much. About my friends, my memories, about everything ending soon. I wanted time to pause. We'd sneak snacks into tuition, gossip during lunch breaks, and get scolded by every teacher possible. I even got caught for copying once — my English teacher looked so disappointed. "Pehal, how could you? You're brighter than this." And I was. I just lost myself for awhile .

I don't know how I survived that year — maybe luck, maybe instincts. Maybe the fire inside me still hadn't died out completely.

But this is what I know now: I am the girl who ate marks like candy. Then I choked on them. Then I spit them out. Then I learned to taste them again — not for the world, not for the iPad, not for the compliments — but for *me.*

Because being brilliant isn't about topping every test. It's about finding your way back when you forget who you are.

And I did.

Chalk Dust and Comebacks

In classrooms buzzing with forgotten math,
She sat with a spark, a comeback path.
A tutor's praise like morning light,
"I'm proud of you" made wrong things right.
Tests got tough, but she held tight.
A bench-mate who laughed when she cried,
Who stayed when others let moments slide.
Ninth grade bloomed in a soft, sweet way—
With flying marks and less cliché.
She learned to show up, come what may.
Then came ten, the myth, the truth,
Of chips at tuition and rebellious youth.
She barely read, she barely slept,
But memories? Those, she proudly kept.
Mistakes were made, but joy was wept.
They called her bright, even when she failed,
Letters copied, tempers derailed.
But still, she stood, loud and flawed,
And in the mess, the teachers applauded.
Because even the rebels get applauded.
Sanskrit first, then boards ahead,
Still French fries danced in her head.
She didn't cram, but she still soared—
A not-so-perfect, perfect board.
A soft storm—loved, feared, adored.

Chapter 4

First Crush, Forever Boy

Dear diary,

It wasn't a silly schoolgirl crush. And even if it started that way, somewhere along the line it grew arms and legs and became a damn tornado.

I don't remember the exact moment, I noticed him., like, Maybe it was his dancing. God, that dancing. When he danced,. In sixth grade, I was on this dumb patrol duty—Drainage Monitor. What a joke. I actually thought I was doing something important, like policing the United Nations of water puddles. And there he was, walking over the drain. My tiny idiot heart decided this was the perfect moment to talk to him. What did I do? I complained. I *actually* went to his class and complained about him, walking over the drain. His soul probably face-palmed from embarrassment. His coordinator made him apologize *to me*, face-to-face. And I remember just standing there, dumbstruck, frozen. I thought it was cool back then. Now I look back and want to crawl under the floorboards.

Then there was that computer class day. I got kicked out for not completing my notes. And while I was sitting outside, head down, pretending to write, he passed by. And guess what I did? I deliberately tilted my notebook, trying to show off my "cute" handwriting, hoping he'd notice. He didn't. Of course, he didn't. He probably didn't even care, and how stupid of me to think, that handwriting was ultimate key to impress someone.

And yet… rumors started. Horrible, stupid rumors. The kind that explode like wildfire in middle school. That we were dating. That I was obsessed. People teased. People laughed. I cried. Because deep down, I always believed that I was an amazingly chaotic person, but that was the first time I looked in the mirror and noticed my scar, my hair, my tone, and somewhere for the first time I felt that I wasn't pretty or enough, first puberty check . I looked in the mirror and saw a scar, saw the dark skin, saw a girl that wasn't pretty enough.

And still, I liked him.

It was never constant—it came in crashing waves.

Sixth grade was the high tide. I didn't like him that badly.OK, plot twist. When this rumour started I didn't like him at that time, really, and I was dating someome in grade six, and yeah after some time we did break up, because he moved to USA. It basically started because I was in general at a moment complementing his dance, and that's where my friends caught me up with that "wanna-be-cool-teenage" thing, teasing or pairing up each other, that constant shipping made me fall head-to-toe for him. Seventh grade? Gone. We had lockdowns, the world shut down, and out of sight became out of mind. Eighth grade, still dry. Ninth? Midterms came and went and suddenly I was back in school. And there he was again. BAM. Tenth grade hit, and I panicked. I tried to shake it off by "liking" someone else. A guy I had been close friends with back in fifth grade—the one I hit with skates, the one who had no clue what was coming. After our last board paper, I ran and confessed to him.

Got rejected. Straight up. No soft landing, no parachute. Just boom.

But that was the moment I knew: I had never really liked him. It was just another poor boy used as a painkiller for a wound I never stitched. I kept forcing myself to move on. To replace one obsession with another, as if that's how hearts worked. It wasn't.

And then came *The Call.*

It wasn't planned. It wasn't sober either. I was riding this high—adrenaline, desperation, madness, I don't even know. I don't remember how I got the courage to actually dial. But I did. And I said it all. That I liked him. That I used to try and impress him with my *attitude.*

And he said—calmly, cuttingly—"Bro, no one's ever impressed by someone's attitude."

Boom. My ego cracked like glass. I had been *so* frank with him, speaking like we were close friends—tu-*tadak* level close, no filters, zero shame, total vulnerability. I sounded like I was drunk on something more than just courage. I felt like throwing my phone straight across the room.

And then I did the stupidest thing of all.

I sent the call recording to my best friends.

They freaked. One was like, "I can't believe you did this. You're not my friend anymore." (of course she was embaressed) Another? Laughed her ass off. I was sitting there, red-faced, heart-broken, clinging to my phone like it could undo what I'd said. But deep down, I wasn't sorry. Not fully. Because it was real. It was *me.* Desperate, messy, unfiltered *me.*

Oh, and the girl who teased me about him in tuition back then?

She's his girlfriend now.

But it stings. I'd be lying if I said it didn't.

You know what hurts the most? Not that he didn't like me. Not that we never became anything. But that I'll always be just the girl who blushed too hard and talked too much and liked him for too long. That I'll always be the one who turned beet-red every time he came close. That I used boys like band-aids and called it healing. That I kept trying to convince myself I was over him, only to fall right back the moment I saw him dance again.

There were pretty bad rumors for a young girl to handle. Heavy ones. The kind a 6th grader shouldn't have had to carry. But I carried them. And the weight shaped me.

I hope he never reads this book.

But I also *really* hope he does.

I somewhere feel we will cross paths again in life, and I hope both of us are available, emotionally, hopelessly, and in every way possible. Call it a gut or an intuition. The way he said on that stupid call that its not your fault trusting the wrong people, I knew it, he was never a "bad choice". People don't tease me anymore, because the time at which I am writing this, it's a long gone crush in their eyes, even I am somewhere over him, but secretly and stating the universal law of all times, you are never over your firsts.

But I'll remember him.

Because he wasn't just a crush...

And he left a mark that no detention slip, no Drainage Monitor badge, and no fake confession could erase. Having a crush—it changes everything. It shifts your perspective on people, on genders, on love itself. Suddenly, you feel seen, wanted, loved, even in tiny, inexplicable ways. And me? I can't hide my feelings. Even when I try, they spill over, all over me. I haven't confessed, not yet, but I know I should be bold enough. Bold enough to say, even if I'm wrong, that yes, this is me, this is what I feel, this is what I did. And it's okay. It's really, really okay.

Those rumours that swirled around me, even though I didn't start them—they've become part of me. And I can't let them go. I don't want to. They mark me, shape me, remind me that feelings are messy, messy but alive, and alive enough to change everything.

Just try to get to know me for once. And I guess it wasn't a 6 grader crush, it was a 4 grader, it was just labelled a not real, or so called feeling. I still wish to meet him.

The Boy I Never Had

I liked you
like the last firework
on a broken Diwali night —
brief, wild,
too bright to forget.
I talked about you
like I knew you.
Wrote poems for a maybe.
Confessed on call recordings,
was teased by my friends,
not to unfriend me for it..
I tried to replace you
with boys I didn't want.
Told one I liked him,
then hated myself
for lying with such aching hope
that you'd finally fade away.
I was stupid. I was bold.
I had no filters,
no shame.
I spoke like we were close —
like we were anything at all.
We never were.

But if you ever read this,

I am sorry.
I am not sorry.
I meant it all.
And I hope we meet.

Chapter 5

Slang, Screens, and Silent Screams

Dear diary,

Grade 6 was that weird little sandwich year — stuck between crayons and concealer, between wanting to grow up and crying for our primary school innocence to come back. I don't even know how to explain it — it was like we were trying on adult shoes that didn't fit but pretending they did. You know that age where you want to feel older, cooler, smarter, but at the same time you miss when your biggest flex was a new scented eraser? Yeah, that was sixth grade. Somewhere deep inside, we all knew it — secondary life had just started, but all we wanted was to rewind. Because primary was... magical. It had its own smells, its own sounds — chalk dust, birthday chocolate bars, brown paper-covered books. But anyway, secondary had begun, and with it,so had the era of chaos.

Grade 7 came in like a storm of screens. I still remember my first online class — Social Studies. I tried to ask a question, spoke for a whole minute, and thought ma'am was ignoring me. Turns out, I was on mute the whole time. That was my grand entry into the online world — a dumb mute mistake. But from that one mistake began an entire revolution. Because Grade 7 didn't just teach me social science — it taught me how to cheat in exams, how to use Zoom, how to fake an audio issue, how to lie with a straight face, how to mute the world and dive into a different one.

And YouTube? That became my best friend. Ashish Chanchlani, Bhuvan Bam, MostlySane, CarryMinati — all the "Not For Kids" stuff I wasn't supposed to watch became my full-time curriculum. I remember attending class in one tab and watching "Types of Teachers" in another. My mom thought I was solving math problems, but I was laughing over roast videos and checking out which Harry Potter character I was in some dumb quiz.

Oh, and speaking of Harry Potter — I finished all eight movies during online school. I used to disconnect my audio and video and escape into Hogwarts while the teacher droned on about agriculture or civics. Exams? Please. I copied so shamelessly, sometimes from Google, sometimes from friends, sometimes from the textbook lying in front of me. Once, I scored 79%, and for the first time in my life, I just didn't care. Like, meh. No guilt. No crying. No overachiever panic. It was just chill.

But here's the thing. As much as pandemic made us lazier, dumber, and extremely creative at cheating — it also gave us something wild. **Time.** So much time. Time to be outside, inside, everywhere, nowhere. Every day after class (or while cthe classes were still on), I'd rush outside. Colony kids would gather by 3 p.m like it was a ritual. Football, cricket, badminton, running around like headless chickens — we played till the sky turned orange and our knees were scraped red. Parents started joining in. Grown-ups playing cricket with us like they were 12 again. It was weirdly beautiful.

You know, sometimes I think the pandemic didn't take our childhood away — it just flipped it, made it louder in some places, and strangely quieter in others. Like, I remember how our parents used to tell us, *"Back in the '90s we used to do this, and that...*" and I swear, one day we just decided — fine, let's do it too. We climbed the *amla* tree in our neighbour's yard just for fun, grabbed those tiny sour bombs, washed them in our kitchen and ate them like treasures. In the evenings, the entire colony felt like a giant playground. Our houses were connected and we jumped — like, actually *jumped* — from house to house, terrace to terrace, hiding behind water tanks during hide-and-seek. The older bhaiyas joined in sometimes. We cycled, played football, and screamed until our voices cracked. I even had this one fight with my mom — and not because I was sleeping in — but because I was waking up *too early*. Like, 6 a.m. early. But not for studying — nah, for *playing*. She wasn't mad, just confused — because every day, as soon as the sun was up, I was out. Gone. At my friend's place, then another friend's, then back at the colony corner where all us girls and boys would gather and turn her guest room into a war zone of laughter and mess. We made reels there, on the lamest trends, and I was obsessed with the chhapri TikTok stars — Riaz Ali, Siddharth Nigam, Arishfa Khan, Avneet Kaur — don't even ask. I had a phase where I'd pout like my life depended on it, waist popping out, thinking I looked like a diva when I just looked like a malfunctioning filter. There was this tacky little hairband I used to wear — I made that poor thing go through every phase with me. And oh my god — my cousin from Pune got stuck with us during the lockdown and she had no choice but to get dragged into my chaos. We did *everything* together — playing for hours at that neighbors place, making cringy TikToks, doing full-blown DIY fashion shows with our moms' sarees and dupattas. Remember there was this best kisser trend on Instagram, no judgements we even did that, like for real. We used to talk *balcony to balcony*, gossiping like grannies. And then rain would hit, and we'd just start dancing in it, barefoot and wild. We made teams for badminton, made *actual* nets, and challenged each other to "rally 50" — who could hit the shuttle 50 times without dropping it. When I look back at it now, I laugh, but somewhere my heart aches a little. Because that version of us — clueless, messy, untamed — was actually magic. Having those bamboo sticks, pepsis, going around the city on our cycles just to feel more big and cool. I remember how my dad and uncles were making us food and were totally proud of it. How can I miss on Ramayans and Mahabharata, the one ritual of every family in that lockdown. I remember me as naughty kid who broke lamps, car mirrors when we were playing football, and everyone laughed their shit out.

I still remember the garden fights — the neighbors who didn't let us play, so we snuck into our friend's house next door and turned their backyard into a stadium. There were days we climbed walls, jumped gates, and pretended we were secret agents. And when the floods came, a bunch of my relatives came to live with us. It was a chaos-filled full house — shared meals, late-night talks, laughter echoing from every corner. I even made my little brother fall off some height once (don't judge), told him to jump and ran away. He hit his head, and I felt like the world's worst human. But I was still the eldest — the unspoken team leader of chaos.

And then there was this friend of mine who lived just a few steps away -diagonal across the street. For 14 days straight, we switched homes. One night at hers, one night at mine. Shared dinners, movie nights, hide-and-seek in the dark. We locked ourselves in almirahs, played dumb charades, had laugh attacks that hurt our stomachs. It was sacred.

Pandemic also brought out our inner bhakts. Like, spiritual bhakts. We did devotional stuff, joined online aartis, sat with our families doing things we usually avoided. Because parents forced us with the classic line: *"This is your age to learn the right thing."* And sometimes, it felt good. Sitting together. Chanting.

Eating prasad. It gave a sense of calm. A strange kind of togetherness.

But the screens... oh god, the screens. We didn't even realize when we became their slaves. We thought they connected us. They disconnected us from reality. My whole world became that one device. I learned to lie, hide, cheat — but also express, explore, escape.

I remember once in Grade 8, I joined the wrong Zoom class by mistake. Thought it was biology, but it was another class. *His* class. My crush. I changed my name, stalked every square box, hoping he'd appear. He didn't. But still, I stayed. Because maybe — just maybe — the universe wanted us in the same digital room for a reason.

At night, we had family group games on WhatsApp. Guess the movie from emojis. Guess the food item from the blurred pic. Silly things, but it kept us close. We laughed. We fought. We were never bored.

During the lockdown, I realized how close I had become to my family. Suddenly, the world outside was paused, but inside, everything was alive. We roamed around the house, ran around the terrace, laughed over the smallest things, even fought sometimes-but always found our way back. I heard my friends say that my mom and chachi were like sisters, and honestly. Family wasn't just family anymore; they were my companions, my friends. Even across cities, we played WhatsApp games together, texting, laughing, competing. Those moments—simple, chaotic, alive—made me realize that sometimes, the people closest to you can be the best friends you will ever have. Even more, during that time, some family from the other part of our city came to live with us because of the floods. And suddenly, I was the eldest sister. I had always craved an older sibling or a cousin closer to me, but being the eldest came with its own kind of privilege. I gotta watch these kids grow, record their little moments, and imagine showing them when they're older: "Look, I captured all of you."

Of course, it wasn't always perfect. Once, I made my little brother stand on a higher step and told him to stay still—he jumped. I still cringe thinking about it. But most of the time, it was magic. I made them dance, play the hop-and-jump games I used to play, laugh at silly things, teach them some tricks—but not everything, because they were already smart enough to figure things out by themselves. And my little sister? She was just… cool. Real, lively, full of energy. I loved every second of being their eldest cousin, their guide, their partner-in-crime, and even their occasional troublemaker.

But the truth? That time's never coming back.

And when schools reopened, it was like culture shock. Offline teachers, real benches, actual chalk. We saw our teachers for the first time — and oh my god, they were wild. There was this English teacher who literally kicked benches. Once he ran behind me and my best friend holding a giant wooden scale. We ran for our lives. Another time, he kicked a guy's backside for whispering. The school felt like a battlefield. And we? We were the soldiers who'd just returned from digital warzones — a little dumb, a little rebellious, and fully wild.

Post-pandemic life was fun, sure. But we lost something. A whole year. Gone. Blank pages in our memory book. Our online friends groups — "Friends Forever," "BFF Gang," "Legends Only" — all felt like something out of a fever dream. Lame, yes. But real.

And through all this — my mom would quietly slide food on my desk during class, thinking she was being sweet. And she was. But I wasn't studying. I was watching Bhuvan Bam kiss a fake girlfriend in some comedy skit. I was lost in the worlds of others because mine felt too confusing.

Pandemic made me learn 50 things, forget 100, and remember the ones that mattered. Like cycling 50 rounds of my colony. Like hiding in closets. Like calling out to friends across balconies. Like watching the sky turn purple while holding a bat in one hand and a half-eaten mango in the other.

We grew together. And we grew apart.

Screens brought us closer. And made us lonelier.

The slang we learned? Stupid. Addictive. Hilarious.

The silence we lived through? Loud as hell.

Things are different now, I want to sit and have those big feasts with my family without any grudge, hoping our parents become those silly little ones again, and truly become someone who we need in our most difficult times, which is now, I wish we should still go on walks with our colony friends and discuss cases and become those lawyers again, still play, break those glasses while playing football in our streets without being scolded, that silly love, urge to be cool but still cry for not having a unicorn pencil. Family became real friends, we saw our dads cooking, moms and grandparents playing, silly fights that didn't last any longer, but somewhere it's long gone. Now the family feels nothing but a "to-do formality list" with money and non- non-negotiable grudge fight train. Before pandemic mornings were slow and nights were long. I still can't process when that little Ms. Pout grew.

I had been given gifts all my life. Not just for topping an exam—sometimes not even for topping, just for doing well, or for trying hard for anything at all. Every little achievement, every little effort, was celebrated with something tangible, something that made me feel seen. And people say that the elder child is the "unloved, responsible one," but that's a myth. Being the first-born has its own pros. You get the pride, the love, the attention—from your parents, your grandparents—even when the younger siblings arrive, It doesn't take that away from you. That love, that feeling of being the first, of being noticed, of being celebrated—it shapes you, quietly, slowly, as you grow, as you mature…sometimes taking far too long to fully understand, but leaving its mark forever.

But yeah.

This chapter — it was something else.

"We didn't waste time — we glitched through it. And somehow, that glitch raised us."

Glitched Childhood, Happy Faces

We woke up to screens, not alarms,
Zoom links, WhatsApp chats, online charms.
School meant typing "Present, Ma'am,"
While hiding YouTube under a cam,
And it was real — even if it wasn't right.
We called our teachers by funny names,
Spammed the chats, played silly games.
Slangs we barely understood,
Made us feel like teens — and it felt good.
Nobody cried — we just didn't care to grow up.
We learned to mute, we learned to lie,
To copy answers and never ask why.
We made fake names, found secret sites,
Watched pranks and Potter till late nights,
This was fun, and it was ours.
It wasn't deep — it was chaos and light,
A glitchy, giggly, glitch-filled delight.
And maybe now we see the cost,
But back then? Not a moment was lost.
If this was childhood — I'm glad it glitched.

Chapter 6

Breaking Rules with Untied Hair

Dear Diary,

I don't even know when the rebellion began. Maybe it was in Grade 6, that day I bunked a class and my coordinator caught me red-handed, and I still stood there like, *"So what? Classes are boring. Make them interesting, then we'll sit."* Okay, bad thing to do. Not nice. But I did it, and I wasn't even sorry then, maybe I am not even now. That was probably where it all started — this slow shift from teacher's pet to "oh no, here she comes." I wasn't the same girl anymore, and honestly, I don't think my mom could've imagined it.

Like when our school elections happened — head boy, head girl were being appointed. Me and my gang of six girls actually went to the vice principal to complain because they were speaking in Hindi. We were like, *"How can you stop us from speaking Hindi if they do it?"* Next day, the principal announces in the assembly that they were scolded. And then, you know what? We continued talking in Hindi anyway. Slangs, double-meaning jokes, all of it. Hypocrites, but proud of it.

And our class — God, our class! We weren't just a group anymore. We were forty people acting like one single brain cell. We were proud softboard monitors. Every month we decorated those boards, like it was our only job— countries as themes, snowman for December, cotton stuck on charts like fake snow. I still remember how we all rushed out during lunch, eating in 15 minutes, escaping teachers just to finish the board. Got scolded so badly, but who cared? Even the guys, who didn't care about anything, sat there cutting snowflakes.

Then came the gathering practice. Contemporary dance, lying on the floor, showing off that I knew the dance better than the choreographer. My class teacher called me out for having an attitude. Next day, the *entire class* had the attitude. During rehearsals we sat in circles playing "situation or truth or dare," debating whether to play veg or non-veg. I swear, we were kids with too many brain cells and no direction. Even our chemistry teacher tried to steal snow from our board to make his class win. Looking back, it was so stupid — but we were happy kids doing happy nonsense.

And once, oh God, the day we turned our benches into a drum set — thak thak thak, clap clap clap. Coordinator told us to stop. Once, twice, thrice — we didn't. He punished us, made us kneel with our hands up in front of the entire building while *Vande Mataram* played. Everyone was staring. My crush was there too. I hid behind people like an idiot. And still, we laughed inside our collars.

We were the so-called "top section" but had zero discipline. Teachers sat girls and boys alternately, thinking they were punishing us. Actually, they united us. Chaos everywhere. We were proud to be drainage monitors, blackboard monitors — like it was some VIP post. Coordinator changed monitors every month so twenty of us strutted around like peacocks. Seniors must've thought we were insane.

Even tuition was rebellion. My bhabhi taught me and I never listened. My elder sister was sincere, but I chilled with friends, failed tests, played with balloons outside instead of studying. I once wrote bio answers on the back of my test book while eating breakfast, planning to cheat. My mom was fed up with my complaints. And the more the teachers complained, the worse I behaved. Me and my three partners-in-crime would deliberately create more chaos just to prove a point.

Grade 9 was where rebellion finally stopped pretending to be cute. You know how in Grade 6 and 7, you think you're a rebel because you sneak your phone under the blanket or skip a homework page? That wasn't real. That was just practice. By Grade 8, the rebelling had become real — laptops and iPads spoiled us like anything. No one was hovering anymore, no moms supervising online classes, no teachers asking for homework every second. Everything was on us, and honestly? I loved it. That strange mix of being treated like an adult but still feeling like a kid — it was addictive.

We weren't angels, not even close. There was this guy who had a crush on one of our friends, and we roasted him to death just because… well, because we could. He wasn't even a bad guy, but we decided he wasn't "good enough," and we were merciless. And then Grade 9 came crashing in — chaos, water fights in classrooms, teachers yelling at us while classmates whispered, "Have a little shame". Like once, me and my best friend were having this insane water fight on her last day in the advanced section. I threw water on her, so did she, we missed each other completely — and soaked this innocent guy standing between us. Oh my god, the way he exploded, "What are you doing?!", dripping wet, while we were apologizing five times a second, trying not to laugh.

Even in Grade 8, most of our teachers couldn't stand us. We'd play dumb games in class, laugh at stupid stuff — like when whitener spilled on one of my male friend's pants. The whole class went crazy with the jokes. The poor guy couldn't even stand up without everyone howling. Teachers would scold us while trying not to laugh themselves. And the hair rule — oh god. Our coordinator had this weird obsession with girls making two braids. Strict orders, no compromises. And obviously, the second we got the chance — like during gathering practice — we'd untie our hair and flip it into ponies. And we had the *best* song for the gathering — proper Bollywood vibes like *Uff Teri Adaa* and *Ilahi* while other classes got stuck with songs no one had even heard of. They were so jealous they started complaining.

Grade 8 was still mid-pandemic, but honestly? It was one of the best years of my life. We were punished more times than I can count. There was this one staircase monitor girl who acted like she owned the school — we used to hate her just for existing, which is ironic because in Grade 6 we were drainage monitors with our own inflated egos. Time really changes you — but also doesn't. Innocence faded, but the core stayed the same. People always say the worst thing a kid can do is wish to grow up fast. They're not lying. That innocence — that way of not knowing how ugly the world can get — you only realize its value after you lose it.

And our school campus —it was pretty huge. Like, actual endless corridors and corners to bunk in. By Grade 9, rebellion was no longer small. It was bold, obvious, in-your-face. Teachers would tell us to do something and we'd do the opposite just because *they* said it. And yeah… I crossed some lines. I made one of my teachers cry. Still one of my biggest regrets. He was actually good, but I was in full "I-don't-care" mode. I told him straight up he wasn't a good teacher. When he asked if he was my favorite, I said no right to his face. I thought I was proving a point. I wasn't — I was just being disrespectful.

The coordinators hated us. They swore me and my two best friends were "spoiling the boys," like girls corrupting innocent guys, not the other way around. Which is hilarious now but back then it pissed me off. We had this giant girls' group — ten, twelve people — and yeah, within that, I had two best friends. One of them was in our coordinator's class, so he adored her but hated me and my other one. Once I actually told him on his face, "Sir, you favor her and always scold us." He almost slapped me. And I was like, "What sir? Show me. Slap me." That's when the hardcore copying phase began. She was always the ones teachers favoured, and obviously we were the one being punished for her sins too. There was this one time when we were running around our building in the morning for some fitness thing our school started and oh god, our school loved CBSEs official site, so it made students do everything they said, and we were the pawns, so, yeah and so were running around, we were like around 4 to 5 girls, and of them tripped like anything, like she was about to fall but the other one caught her and the one who caught her saw that she was laughing so she let go off her, but then I caught her and somehow I was also about trip, but somehow balanced, and this confusing but epic scene was witnessed by our other friends who were walking through the doors in front of the building, our basketball coach saw and he punished us for no reason, again THE THREE OF US, and then made us run in around 100 rounds of a dome shaped area, okay, yes it was pretty small, but around 100 runs for a nonsense thing, that did even seem intentional, but yes it was the OG LUCK that lasted pretty long, and she the teacher's favourite one was sent and we kept running and begged him to even leave us, but guess what he didn't leave us and made the two of us ran till the second last stage of asthama.

I didn't even pretend to keep up. In Grade 8 at least I *had* an English notebook — half empty, but there. In Grade 9? No social science books at all. No history, no geography, no civics, no economics. Nothing. Me and the guy behind me would divide the syllabus like criminals. He studied half, I studied half, then we'd swap answers in exams. We didn't even bother to copy discreetly — full pages written in different words with the same meaning.

My benchmate — one of my closest friends in Grade 9 — she stood by me through every bad move. When I threw a stapler at someone, when I mouthed off to teachers, when I got dragged to the vice principal's office for not making my notebooks — she never flinched. Once, we even made a teacher cry just because we didn't have our books. He literally took us to the VP crying. Over notebooks. And still, she sat there with me, taking the heat.

Grade 9 was also where first relationships started popping up. My benchmate got her first boyfriend and we hated him… until they broke up. Don't judge us, we were kids. Then two of our other friends started dating and it became this weird double-date thing happening in the corridors. Of course, they got caught — teachers actually clicked pictures of them and posted complaints on the school app. Peak SGI scandal.

Me and my other friend were in the same tuition, cycling there every day, spending money on junk food instead of books, watching stand-up comedy on my iPad instead of studying. We did everything but the actual work — except physics. Physics was the only thing we took seriously. And there was this teacher — we called her the "train announcer" because of her voice. We'd mimic her constantly and always got caught. Once, we were late returning from the washroom, and the coordinator and chemistry teacher caught us and literally called us "gorillas." He compared us to monkeys running for bananas when the bell rang.

We pulled off so much nonsense I can't even write about all of it. Some things were bad. Like, really bad. But then there were the funny ones — like this PTM when our deputy vice principal asked me to call my mom because he wanted to complain. So I brought my friend's mom instead. Sir thought she was my mom, she thought It was her daughter the sir was talking about, and my friend was dying trying to stop my mom from walking in. When sir realized the mix-up, he went ballistic: "Your mother, idiot! YOUR mother!" I got scolded worse, but my real mom took my side because I was killing it at sports, extracurriculars, and still passing exams somehow. I was in my prime.

We played Holi in the school bus, blasted retro songs one day, Hanuman Chalisa the next. The bus maushi would scream at us but we didn't care. Once we bunked during a sports event to get ice creams and drinks — forbidden to be on the ground, obviously — and got chased by the math HOD and vice principal. We gaslighted them for a while but eventually got caught red-handed by our coordinator. He took our picture while we were trying not to laugh.

We were "the cool kids". Skipping school for movies, driving around without telling our parents, watching friends sneak into other cities during tuition hours. There was even this guy who got punished so badly they made him guard the main gate, opening and shutting it for everyone like a watchman. We were out of control — lying, scamming, disrespecting, and loving every second of it.

Grade 9 was the year everything stopped feeling like a joke. You know how in Grade 6 or 7 you *think* you're rebelling because you skip homework or watch YouTube in class? That's not rebellion. That's training wheels. By Grade 8, it was real — we were completely unsupervised, spoiled by our iPads and laptops, free to make our own decisions… and our own mess. And I loved that phase. I loved being trusted like an adult but still laughing like a kid. That messy in-between where nobody's holding your hand but you haven't let go of your innocence yet.

This is the time I realized I don't want to grow up really. But, this is also the the time that I realized that I have so much more amazing stuff coming my way in I adulthood. Just with a pinch of spices to it you know.

The years we didn't listen

We thought rebellion was just a game,
In Grade 6 and 7, it never had a name.
Laptops, iPads, freedom on our own,
Grade 8 hit harder—our wildness had grown.
We mocked bad crushes, untied our hair,
Teachers scolding, but we didn't care.
Whitener jokes, songs that made them mad,
A big campus to bunk—childhood going bad.
By Grade 9, rules were ours to break,
Told a teacher he's not good—my mistake.
No notebooks made, no lessons done,
Copying in exams, still called number one.
Benchmates loyal through every fight,
Boyfriends, ships, kisses in plain sight.
Coordinators chasing, calling us wild,
But I was untouchable—a fearless child.
Bus rides in color, music at dawn,
Holi in corridors, innocence gone.
We lied, we bunked, we gaslit too,
Believing whatever we did was true.

Chapter 7

When Fights Made Me Famous

Dear diary,

I wasn't born a fighter. I was born a crier. The kind of kid who would burst into tears, play the victim card, and secretly laugh when the other person got scolded for something that didn't even hurt me. That used to be my superpower — I didn't need to throw punches when I could throw tears.

But something changes when you grow up. Somewhere between the fake proudness of Grade 6 and 7 and the real rebellion of Grade 8 and 9, I stopped being scared of confrontation. If I was wrong, I'd still argue. If I was right and you tried to put me down, I'd fight. And when I fought, I didn't whisper.

One thing about me — I stand for my people. Always. Even if they're wrong, even if they're reckless, even if I know they don't deserve it that day. I'll fight for them, cover for them, protect them like they're mine. A lot of my friends don't even know about half the fights I've picked up for them. And that's fine. I don't do it for credit. I do it because loyalty is my love language.

I yelled at classmates who wouldn't stop teasing my best friend. I clashed with coordinators who thought girls were always the bad influence in mixed groups. I called out anyone who thought could walk over me or my people. I wasn't subtle. I didn't care who I was fighting — teacher, senior, "popular kid", anyone.

Words spread fast. Suddenly I wasn't just the "bright kid" or the "sports girl" or "the one who wins prizes." I was the girl who would stand up for anyone — and never back down. People said I was fearless. Honestly, I was just done being quiet.

Fights made me famous, not because I won them all, but because I didn't care if I lost — as long as no one touched my people.If you love someone, you show it. You don't bottle it up inside, don't let it sit quietly in your chest. You show them. Make them feel it—how much they matter, how much they are loved, how much they are seen. That's one of the greatest gifts you can give someone, especially someone with attachment issues, someone who already has everything but still craves being valued.

And you don't have to follow the crowd. If your friends don't like someone, you don't like them either. That's what girlhood taught me: it is peakhood. The freedom, the intensity, the honesty of it—there is nothing higher, nothing better.

I Don't Fight Alone

I wasn't born to swing my fists,
I was born to cry and twist,
To play the victim, shed a tear,
Let someone else absorb the fear.
But somewhere, growing made me loud,
No longer lost inside the crowd.
If I was wrong, I'd argue still,
If I was right, I'd bend my will.
I fight for mine — my chosen crew,
Even if they're wrong, I'll see it through.
I don't need thanks, I don't need fame,
I'll take the heat, I'll take the blame.
From classrooms, buses, PTMs,
To coordinators' angry hems,
I yelled, I stood, I drew the line,
Not for glory, but because they're mine.
You can call me fearless, wild,
A loyal heart, a stubborn child —
I don't fight for crowns or throne,
I just refuse to fight alone.

Chapter 8

Farewell with Flooded Eyes

Dear diary,

Grade 10 felt like standing at the edge of two worlds — one where you're still a kid, eating lunch in the corridor, laughing over stupid jokes, and another where suddenly you're supposed to be a grown up, deciding streams, careers, and "what will you become in life." It's funny, because I've always said I love change. I love moving forward, exploring, starting fresh. But the irony? I never want the people around me to change. I want my home to stay the same. I want my people to stay the same. So when Grade 10 came, it hit me in ways I wasn't expecting. Because Grade 10 was the kind of change where not only the year changed, but *I* changed. And not just intellectually — with exams, syllabus, competitive pressure — but emotionally, too.

This was the year I actually started having **friendship dramas**. I know, late bloomer alert. By this time, all my friends were basically veterans at betrayal. They'd had their "he said–she said," their "she stole my best friend," their "we don't talk anymore" phases. Some had boyfriends, some had already tasted heartbreak, some had already been through the whole soap opera of high school. And me? I was still stuck at square one. Grade 10 was like, "Girl, it's your turn now." So yeah — friendship breakups, betrayals, people leaving, people returning — all of it landed on me for me at once. And I wasn't ready.

See, before this, if I wasn't friends with someone anymore, it was never dramatic. It was always, "Corona happened, we drifted apart, life moved on." Like my Grade 5 best friend — we didn't fight, we didn't betray, we just… faded. But Grade 10? No, it wasn't that soft. It was loud, messy, complicated. The first time I actually felt what it meant to be *hurt by a friend*. The first time I realized you could love someone like family and still break apart like strangers. And maybe it was late for me, but late or not, it hit harder than I thought.

And honestly? It shaped me. The girl who once swore she'd never cry, started crying. A lot. Over people. Over friendships. Over small things I would've once laughed off. And it's not something I'm proud of — I don't romanticize crying. But it did make me softer, more emotional, more sensitive in ways I hadn't allowed myself to be before. In a weird way, Grade 10 cracked me open. It showed me that strength isn't always about holding back tears, sometimes it's about letting them fall.

And logistically, Grade 10 itself was just… different. Like, even the way we were split up. I was in **A Section** — the only section on the first floor. The rest of the nine sections? Ground floor. Which basically meant that half my friends were downstairs living their best lives while I was stranded upstairs with people I barely vibed with. Even my bench partner — who became my best friend in Grade 9— ended up leaving. She didn't want to continue in the "advanced" section, so she shifted out. Which left me stuck with two girls, me and my bench partner used to constantly bitch about. The irony was insane. One of them was the classic two-faced friend — all smiles in front of you, but fake behind your back, but honestly though I am saying this about her, we actually had quiet crazy moments and trust me even I was no good to her, it's both way around you know, so no blame games. The other… I liked her but she was that girl's best friend..so.

But if there's one thing that saved me in A Section, it was the **boys**. The boys in my class have always been my **A1 since day one**. My constants. My chaos buddies. Even when the girl drama got messy, they were the ones who made me laugh, who made the class feel lighter. They were my survival kit.

At first, I hated being in A Section. I wanted to shift downstairs with everyone else. But eventually, I realized that being physically apart didn't break my friendships — it actually made them stronger. Like, if anything, it made us miss each other more. My friends would run upstairs during breaks just to see me, and I'd sneak down to the ground floor whenever I could. The distance wasn't distance — it was a reminder that people will walk for you if they want to.

And that's how we bonded harder. We bunked classes together, laughed about teachers, roasted each other about nicknames. Like, my teacher once called me a **monkey**, and another friend got labeled a **tomboy**, and those became inside jokes for weeks. We'd huddle and gossip about how some teacher slapped someone, or how another teacher made fun of someone's walk. It was reckless, messy, full of energy — the kind of chaos you can only get in school corridors.

Our group itself was iconic — 10 to 12 girls, no boy drama, just pure girl gang energy. And I swear, you haven't seen chaos until you've seen 12 girls trying to walk together to the **bus bay**. Our bus bays were far from the school building, and technically, we were supposed to walk in neat, class-wise lines. But somehow, every single day, we managed to walk together. Like one giant parade of madness. We'd wait for each other, make space, pull people in. And those bus bay walks? They were the highlight of my day. It's not like we didn't had groups with our male friends, actually that was the one we used to hangout with, the main ones, but this one, all girls, only fun, like the other main group you know.

And the **bus journeys** — don't even get me started. They were where we laughed the loudest, where secrets got spilled, where "you had to be there" moments happened. I had my best friend by my side, the windows down, hair flying, music playing on someone's phone. Those rides home were our therapy.

And then there were the **sports days and interhouse matches**. We'd fight over teams, yell at each other during the game, argue like enemies. But as soon as the match ended, we were the first to run and hug the player, cheer them, scream their name. That's the thing about our group — we could fight like brothers but love like sisters too.

Even our **gathering practices** hit different. In Grade 10, we didn't have to participate like before, so we got to sit back and just... watch. Watch the chaos of other grades, laugh at their steps, secretly enjoy the freedom of not being in the spotlight. And the **teacher errands** — oh god. Don't even count how many times we were caught running down corridors with files, or how many times coordinators rolled their eyes at us. The funniest part? Among hundreds of students, the vice principal somehow only remembered **my name**. So every time something happened, I was the one being yelled at.

Grade 10 was also the year I caught feelings again — for my **Grade 5 best friend**. Don't ask me why. Life is weird like that. Sometimes people circle back into your story in ways you don't expect.

But beneath all the chaos, Grade 10 was about growth. About realizing that sometimes, the people you thought you'd hate become tolerable. That the friends you thought you'd lose forever fight to stay. That betrayal stings, but loyalty heals. That change is scary, but sometimes it takes you exactly where you need to go.

It was fried rice — a mix of everything. Bits of sweet, bits of salty, bits of spice. The kind of dish where nothing matches, but together, it somehow works.

I won't lie — I was the bitch this time. I was the wrong one. And admitting that even now feels like swallowing glass. It didn't happen overnight; it started with tiny cracks. My best friend's guy best friend joined our school that year. On day one, they fought. She cried. He sulked. I didn't know him, but I was furious. Day two, I saw him outside my class and snapped — "How dare you make her cry?" I yelled so loud he nearly tripped onto the teacher's table. He stammered apologies, and by evening he sent me a Snapchat request. I accepted, apologized back, and somehow — the three of us became great friends. Midnight calls, endless conversations. People even whispered he liked me, but I brushed it off. To me, he was just a friend. A great friend.

But then came the mess, and me, with my sarcasm sharp as glass, snapped, "Dude…" He mistook it. He went back and told her. She called me, her voice cracking: "Did you really say that? How could you?" I swore I didn't mean it, swore it was sarcasm, but the damage was done. From then, the fights multiplied.

And then I did the worst thing: I chose sides. No one gave me a choice, but I made one anyway. I started ignoring her, started drifting away, started clinging to another best friend just because it felt easier. I left behind the girl who always reciprocated my energy, the girl who came back from her hometown just to show up at my surprise birthday party on August 14th. And what did I give her? Excuses. Tears on command. Playing the victim every time she confronted me.

Friendship Day made it worse. I told her boyfriend something I thought was harmless, just "friend advice", again I didn't mean it. It blew up. The next day, she didn't talk to me. She looked me in the eye and said the words that shattered me: "I don't think we're best friends anymore."

And that's when I realized, I didn't only break her, but even myself. I begged, I cried, I chased her for a whole year. I tried keeping contact, tried being in her orbit, even when deep down I knew I had lost her. I lost a gem while clinging to stones. And yet, on the farewell day, when my eyes were drowning, she was the one who came up from behind and hugged me. She whispered, "It's okay. We'll still be friends." In that second, my heart shattered and healed all at once.

She was one of the greatest friends I've ever had. Even now, I don't want her back in my life the way she once was — but I'll always adore the version of her that existed in my past. The girl who cared. The girl who stayed. The girl who deserved far more than what I gave her.

And here's the part I hate admitting: I still stayed friends with her ex. Not close, just hi-bye in groups. He was never someone close, but at least he was "good" to me Maybe that was selfish. Maybe that was the real proof that I was the villain in her story.

Still, I did one thing right: I cursed and unfollowed and, cut the other one off. I wasn't going to repeat my mistakes again. Yet I won't disagree, that he was a great and a genuine friend to me who spoke for me in the room, the other one, but that doesn't matter, because now I knew the girl is my priority, and we were friends because of her.

Yes, I was selfish. I was cruel. I was the bitch. But I was also just a teenager — fumbling, insecure, desperate to belong. Teenagers do stupid things. Hurtful things. Unforgivable things.

Sometimes you have to live through being the worst version of yourself before you can grow into someone better.

But god, did we have fun. Real fun. Messy, chaotic, unforgettable fun. We weren't just a group, we were a gang — ten, sometimes twelve of us, roaming around like we owned the school. While boys usually got that reputation, this time it was us girls. We were loud, dramatic, always in trouble.

Like the day we got punished for being late to class. The teachers made us stand in the assembly area and sing a prayer before we were allowed back. Simple enough. Except when it was my turn, I blanked. Started chanting "Guru Brahma, Guru Vishnu," forgot halfway, switched to another one, forgot that too. I finally threw my hands up and told sir, "Just let me go, I don't remember any prayers." That was me in Grade 10 — unapologetically ridiculous.

And yet, those days had magic. I was the third wheel with my two closest friends, but I didn't even mind. There was laughter, bunking, whispers about elections. I hadn't even planned on standing for student elections, but I did anyway. Lost — apparently by five votes, with everyone blaming teacher favoritism. Whatever. The best part was bunking seven, eight lectures just to campaign and yell "vote for me!" across corridors.

Our campus was a world in itself. Huge, sprawling, impossible to cover in one day — but me and my best friend tried anyway. Just before boards, we came back a few days early and ditched the study sessions. Instead, we walked. Everywhere. Kindergarten, primary, football ground, swimming pool, basketball court. Every corner had a memory — "Remember when we got caught here? Remember when you cried here? Remember when I embarrassed myself here?" We laughed until our stomachs hurt. At one point, we sneaked into the

Cambridge section, got caught, ran like fugitives, dodged teachers in elevators, and even lied that "sir sent us" — when the sir didn't even know we existed. That day was freedom. That day was life.

And I swear, we weren't doing it for Instagram. No time-lapses, no stories, no filters. Just being kids. Just living.

But we weren't limited to school. After prelims, buses dropped us at common spots, so one day, me, her, and two guys ended up near her house and decided, in full uniform, to walk into a café. Chilling as if we nailed the examinations, then walking for ice creams, then the other rode him back , going to soda shops, talking on a far off location, so that me and my best friend could have a good walk and spill the daily tea. Like me and her most were around each other most of the time. Be it in tuitions, cafe hopping hours, buses, bunks, our duo study sesh where we ended up scrolling Snapchat, lying around each other's places, clicking snaps to show we are also the ones growing. Even on calls after coming home, like grade 8, 9, and 10 were really our years. I Remember her dad telling us to rent a flat in their new building.

Like if you know her, you have to know MOTHER TAYLOR SWIFT, so we even went to "THE ERAS TOUR" movie, like just the two of us, unknowingly living in girlhood. We shared everything, like everything. The instagram coded best friends, even spilling about their familys, every firsts, thinking about when to tell them this happened, we were just going with the flow, enjoying and crying at the same about growing up. One of my favorite instances was, when I told her "I love how the sky looks today",she immediately sent a picture of it every angle. Lived peak girlhood without even knowing about it.

Even tuition was chaos. Supposed to be "study sessions," but we barely studied. Four hours meant one hour of books, three hours of nonsense. One friend even lit a matchstick and threw it at a teacher, claiming it was a prank. He was scolded half to death, but I laughed for hours. We prank called our teacher, watched phones, made relatable memes And then there was our bio teacher. Two years of suffering under her microscope, literally and metaphorically. I don't even know what personal grudge she had against us, but I swear she carried it like a badge. We were in that dreaded reproduction chapter—by then, honestly, we knew every single line by heart. There was nothing funny, nothing new, nothing giggle-worthy left in it. But she decided otherwise. She was convinced we were laughing, mocking, doing some childish nonsense, and she went off on us. Half an hour straight. Not even a pause for breath. And the funniest part? We weren't even guilty. We were sitting there with a group of girls from the other section, dead serious, and they turned out to be the worst kind of backstabbers. Big fat liars, nodding along with her, saying, "Yes, ma'am", "they were laughing"," ma'am, they were disturbing the class". My jaw almost hit the desk. After she left, we went and narrated the real story to our teacher, every detail, because honestly, we couldn't just swallow that humiliation.

And then there was this one girl from my section—one of those rare constants, not anymore but yeah, who made Grade 10 bearable. She was the best friend of that other girl, but with me, she was different. We had our own little world. Cycling together, wasting tuition hours not on books but on stand-up comedy clips I smuggled in on my iPad, sharing chips like they were secret treasure. She didn't have a cycle, so I'd walk beside her, pushing mine all the way from the tuition to her house, carrying the weight of the cycle but never once feeling it because the conversation was enough. I still remember us laughing in the corridors, sneaking moments during basketball, finding excuses to just linger around each other. She was real, she was present, and even now, she's still that—someone I can look back at and say, yeah, "we were good friends", and maybe we still are.

It started with a limp. A minor injury from football that should've healed in days turned into a small tear, and suddenly I was the girl who couldn't move. Two, three days of bed rest at home, then more inside school walls — but not in the way you'd expect. My food was sent from the mess to my classroom. didi's carried dal, chawal, rotis with that quiet kindness only they could manage. And there I sat: a whole building to myself, empty corridors, empty rooms, just me. It felt like a haunted version of "Home Alone", except the ghosts were boredom and silence .

The second day, I couldn't take it. I asked one of my closest friends — my so-called fifth best friend — to stay back with me. Lunch was thirty-five minutes; he gave me twenty of them. Just the two of us, in an empty building, talking about nothing and everything, while the world outside kept spinning. What made it stranger was how much my class teacher — my ideal, the man I respected most — trusted me. Trusted us. In a school where people had been caught doing things they shouldn't behind closed doors, he never doubted me. "Talk to her, then go eat", he said, and walked away. That trust was heavier than any punishment.

Grade 10 made me reckless in ways I can't regret. The very next day, I pulled one of my most ridiculous pranks. On the board, in my coordinator's handwriting — or close enough to fool half the class — I scribbled: All science students must stay for an orientation till 7 p.m. The panic was instant. "I'm commerce!" "I'm arts!" Everyone begged to be exempt. Half the class was convinced, the other half laughed because they knew only I would dare. When my teacher found out, he smiled instead of scolding. "If you don't do this now, then when will you?" he said. That was the magic of Grade 10. Our teachers knew we were misbehaving, but sometimes even they wanted us to live it out.

It wasn't just fun. Opportunities poured in too — a quiz to Uzbekistan that got cancelled because of COVID, two AFS rounds for USA and Japan, all of them brushing against my fingertips before slipping away. That was also the year I decided I would take science, a decision that was both my worst mistake and my best choice. I dreamed of IIT not for engineering, but for its brand. The name, the aura, the thought of attending e-summits and fashion shows on that campus — it lit me up. I never really cared about JEE; I cared about the feeling of being there. And physics, especially, felt like mine — thanks to the teacher who made it less of a subject and more of a religion.

Sports kept me equally restless. Football politics taught me what it meant to earn something. Girls came to me whispering about who deserved captaincy, who didn't, and I realized I had a voice that mattered, people looked at me as someone who could change the game. That recognition was intoxicating. My friends calling me state level captain was one of the best feelings ever.

But if sports gave me respect, my own stupidity balanced it out. On 13th March — the day boards ended — I walked up to my fifth grade best friend and blurted out a confession: I like you. He laughed. Thought it was a prank. When he finally realized I was serious, he just said, "Thank you." I asked, "So... do we do something about it?" and he shrugged: I don't know. Not sure. That was the moment I knew it wasn't real. I didn't actually like him. I just wanted to bury the ghost of someone else. Wanted validation. Wanted distraction. While trying to replace one boy with another, I ended up replacing honesty with lies.

A gallery of chaos, and nowhere was it clearer than our science exhibition. I was being scolded left and right—complaints always following me like shadows—but somehow, that only made the day sweeter. The exhibition coincided with the parent-teacher meeting, and as usual, my mother was ready to defend me, balancing praise with the usual parental frustrations about my "third-class behavior". Meanwhile, my friends and I were in our own universe, upstairs in the assembly area, cameras ready, capturing my crush in every possible angle—because that's what girlhood looks like: plotting, giggling, and documenting every stolen glance.

When the principal didn't show up on time, panic hit the group. One friend whispered that he had arrived, and I froze—I wasn't ready. But somehow, I was saved from scrutiny by the timing of fate, or maybe by the universe conspiring with my friends. That day became a collage of memories: making pencils dance like garba sticks, snapping endless pictures, gossiping with reckless delight, and laughing until our stomachs hurt. In those moments, nothing else existed but the joy of being with your people, doing your thing, breaking rules in tiny, magical ways, and knowing that this—right here, will be something we'll always carry.

It will always golden in my mind. Even when my Sanskrit teacher hated me for gossiping. Even when prelims turned into a circus of missing books, falling off chairs, and pretending to study while secretly plotting after-school cafés in uniform. Even when I played the fool, I never felt more at home. These friends — the ones I sat with, laughed with, made reels with, got caught by police with — they made me believe I had a place. That even if everything else crumbled, I could fall back into their arms and still belong.

So yes, 95% and 98% may look the same on a report card. But they're not the things I cry about now. I cry about those corridors, those afternoons, those teachers who trusted me when I didn't trust myself. I cry about the pranks, the laughter, the stupid confessions. The academics faded. The memories stayed.

And then came August 14th—a day that will always live in my memory like some perfect, chaotic little storm. I had been suspicious because, well, it wasn't my birthday; my birthday was in May. But my mother, in her quiet, fierce way, had planned the most beautiful surprise birthday for me. And the best part? My best friend, my bench partner, had come all the way back from her hometown just for me, just to make sure I felt seen. I still remember that morning—the little conspiracies between my mother and her, the whispered planning, the tiny lies to keep me from figuring it out. My mother, the ever-loving strategist, had even warned me, "She's cunning, don't let her know you know." And I didn't.

Invitations, decorations, little gifts—everything was ready before I even realized it. My friends had done it all, my mother had done it all, and I was just the unsuspecting center of it. It was perfect. And yes, knowing me, chaos followed me everywhere. That night, as I went home, running late, we got stopped by the police—my friends and I, laughing, panicking, trying to explain ourselves. But nothing could dim the magic of that day. We had run through mazes, made teachers chase us like we were some wild story unfolding in real life, and my friends—the three boys who were somehow both terrifying and protective—kept me laughing the entire time. Somewhere in that mess, I even lost my captaincy badge, and it didn't matter. Nothing mattered.

Then the farewells hit, and everything went off the rails. Three, four parties—class farewell, group farewells, one where exes were dancing and we couldn't stop laughing. Late-night games, draw-wise chaos, my best friend coming up with all these insane ideas, The post-board era was golden, no rules, no guilt. I was running from dance practice to turf to movies, roaming India, doing everything I could think of, every single second. Peak girlhood of getting ready in the washrooms, forcing guys to make reels, go karting like we could literally die next moments running those cars in bushes, the dance, car rides, the music banging, everything revolving around us.

Sleepovers were sacred rituals—dancing until dawn, terrace Maggi at 4 a.m., watching the sunrise, swearing no one sleeps before the first light. We laughed, we cried, we fought, we made dreams under the sky. Snapchat streaks, Instagram stories, food experiments, spilled teas, spilled pizzas, first bites of sushi, waffles, ice cream—you name it, we lived it. Even small things felt infinite, that we all got somewhere tattooed on us.

Playing drawize and among us with amigos till 4 at night, even after having an all day long hangout. Group calls went from 1 to 4 hours, nothing just all those bitchy stupid talks.

Holi in Mahabaleshwar was madness—colors flying, laughter everywhere, chaos in the air, Mahesh bhavan Holi dance being there, and yes, my sixth-standard crush popping at the worst moments, making me blush, making me alive. One of my friends waited to see my dance there and then disappeared, said had some work. I was worst dressed that day, in front of him, but it's okay who cares.

Parents were anchors in the storm. My mom—quietly fierce, showing love through actions, never saying it, but proving it. My dad—emotionally distant but always saying yes, teaching me to chase what I wanted, even if the path was blocked. I wanted Manali, friends backed off, but my mom, the best person ever, my dad said no to not go for treks to Manali, but my mom, pulled every contact, close or distant, making me have that one dream fulfilled of mine, she always tried, just in some other way people don't expect, but she always hears the voice of my heart. The only person who's loved me unconditionally, without making it count on anything is her. I really wish I am the reason she always smiles and always protects her from ones who play two faced. I love her more than anything.

Those days were chaos incarnate: barefoot runs in sayaji, go-karting with four guys while my best friend and I drove recklessly, flipping into bushes, everyone screaming. Car rides with music blasting, hotel washrooms turned into makeup dens, McDonald's runs, dancing, laughing, crying at goodbyes. People we hated became friends, secrets spilled, pranks went wrong, police caught me late at night. None of it mattered—we were living. Too many photos, with too many people.

Friendship nicknames stuck—Papa ki Pari, Junglee, bro—driving, eating, hanging out, every second counted. Birthdays became bashes, reels forced on boys, selfies clicked endlessly, crushes observed secretly, hearts racing. That chaotic era was a mix of laughter, tears, adrenaline, nostalgia.

The best journey I could have asked for—a year that tested me, shaped me, and left me with lessons I will carry forever. I grew in ways I didn't expect, not by becoming "completely mature," but by realizing that true maturity is knowing when to switch it on. It's okay to be carefree, to laugh and stumble and make mistakes, but when the situation demands it, you must stand firm, think clearly, and face it with strength.

I learned that people matter—their presence, their efforts, their quiet ways of showing up when you least deserve it the least . You should never be the reason behind someone's tears, nor should you abandon them in their weakest moments. There's a fine line between being self-centered and being self-obsessed, and it's important to know the difference. Respect is not optional—it defines you more loudly than words. Disagree in your head if you must, roll your eyes silently, but never cross into disrespect, whether with teachers, peers, or anyone. Behavior speaks louder than marks or achievements ever could. Even when my 10th results came out, I was a little crushed seeing my science marks—they were way lower than I expected. I knew I could've done better, especially after all the nonsense and distractions I'd gotten myself into. My mom didn't say much, but I could sense a tiny flicker of disappointment—she knew my potential, and somewhere, she had expected more. But even then, my entire family was over the moon. Everyone was proud, so proud of me. My relatives, my friends, even people I hadn't spoken to in ages—they called and congratulated me. And somehow, despite my own disappointment, their joy made me feel seen, celebrated, loved. It was overwhelming, in the best way.

I realized that fun and responsibility don't cancel each other out. Hanging out with friends, creating chaos, dancing in the rain—it's all beautiful. But so is making a strong academic or sports comeback. Both matter, both make you proud. And if there's one rule Grade 10 carved deep into me, it's this: never date within your friend group. It ruins everything. Friendships are too precious to gamble like that.

It was more than just a year; it was my teacher, my stage, my mirror. It taught me things I never thought I would learn, and even more, it made me live through moments I never thought I would survive. Crying is cool too.

I don't remember my marks right now, but wherever I am right now it's all because of my confidence, a nerdy nature that once haunted me down there.

That group, those friends, that chaos—it formed after grade ten, unexpected, unplanned, but permanent. Forever stamped on my heart.

Infinity

It was the last year,
Eyes full of quiet tears,
Heart split between hope and hurt,
We knew it won't last forever,
Chillax. Take a wine
Even ending deserves a line.

They say, "every ending is a new beginning",
But this one? It was too loud. Too full,
It took a whole year,
Just to begin again.
And even then, it still felt like a goodbye.

We were the final chapters of us,
Deadly worried,
But still showing up.

Playing and crying,
Laughing and breaking,
being witchy, being bitchy-
Putting on performances we never rehearsed,
But somehow nailed.

We carried it all,
Some drifted behind- not forever,
Just far enough to miss.

We walked apart,
Hand in hand,
Not all paths aligned.
The journey sped up, the grip loosened,
(And no, physics wasn't our subject,
But we kept understanding the falling).

Hands changed,
Smiles shifted,
pretense rose,
But we held on,
Not forever-
But long enough.

Yes there were double faces,
Too many, too fake,
Yet, we accepted it all.

Class ten was a trailer
The world? The full film.
But the worst kinda people?
We already met the worst one,
And somehow,
Made it out.

Chapter 9

Left Behind at 11

Dear diary,

Grade 11 hit me like a storm I wasn't ready for. My best friend left for Pune, and suddenly the group of four I had relied on felt like it might crumble overnight. My other so called amigos took admission in SGIS Jr. collage, so almost half of the people were there, altogether. I was left to navigate this new world alone, in a college that felt less like a place to learn and more like a cage. Not literally a jail, but close enough—stifling, suffocating, draining. The corridors were half the width of my old school's, the classrooms were packed, students spilling onto the floors, the washrooms crowded like some chaotic market. Breaks were non-existent. Meals, optional. Freedom, a myth.

The first day of college felt like a bad omen dressed up as an orientation. A management head who should have been greeting us instead screamed at a roomful of fresh faces until half the auditorium emptied. Where school had been a messy, generous chaos, this place was clinical and tight, a cage stacked with chairs and rules. Three classes on one floor, a single tiny washroom that had to serve a hundred and fifty people in two short breaks — simple logistics made everything feel oppressive. The corridors were narrower than a slice of the school I came from; the air tasted like someone else's fear. I remember thinking, "This is going to be a test of endurance." I didn't realize how personal that test would become.

Out of that weird, cramped beginning, friendships began not because of history but because of need. I met her — the girl who would become the pivot of the year — through a mutual. She slid into my classroom like a bookmark, someone I'd only just met but who fit into a paragraph of my life so quickly it looked written in ink. With another girl from my school (the one who eventually came to "E4"), the three of us formed a desperate trio: two college transfers and one old acquaintance stitched together by lunchtime conspiracies and the raw hunger to belong. Desperate friendships are honest in a way regular friendships sometimes aren't — they confess their loneliness with less ceremony — and for a while, that rawness felt like enough.We navigated the rules—boys and girls weren't allowed to talk openly, but we found loopholes, connections, and made our own world inside theirs. Mutual friends, shared jokes, football matches, silly games.

I built myself a small, chaotic world: turf evenings, late-night video calls with the friend who moved to Pune, impromptu waffle deliveries, "come for ten minutes" rescue missions when someone needed an escape. I would call them last-minute for Friendship Day and they would come — every time — because we were the kind of people who turned up. We made Navratri into our own carnival: thirty people screaming and dancing, glitter in our hair, choreography of belonging. I planned things on the fly; they showed up. Those little spontaneous loves — waffles at dawn, shoes kicked off for barefoot runs, three-a.m. rooftop Maggi — felt like proof that some things would stay.

Then the fissures started. It usually happens that way: a misstep, then a rumor, then a silence that grows teeth. My mutual — the one who had been new and bright — began to tilt. Floors shuffled, sections changed, and with those small institutional moves, loyalties shifted. She started answering differently. She began to pull away. At first I blamed logistics and distance, until

I realized she had quietly chosen other anchors. The worst part: she didn't simply drift. She pitched something about me in front of the group, a line that turned out to be poison. Suddenly, I was the outsider in the only circle that had felt like home. The betrayal stung more because she had never been my childhood friend — she was a stranger who had walked straight into the shape of my trust and then shattered it. She's a bitch that 's all I want to say.

I tried to fix it. I wrote letters, called until my throat hurt, explained myself until words ran thin. For months I chased a version of friendship that existed only in my head: the girl who had shown up at my surprise birthday because my mother and her had planned it together, who had once stood in the middle of a small conspiracy to make me cry happy tears. But her "funny tone" on a group call — "I don't think we're best friends anymore" — was a sentence that sounded like a verdict. It turns out you can be left behind even while people keep taking your pictures and tagging you. I learned that people sometimes keep you in a sentimental archive while building a present that no longer has room for you. Her fake assuring, lying to me and just after a single misunderstanding, ditching me and then saying to me "I have always been more close to my guy friends", made her doubt the bind we shared in the past. She made me feel pathetic and a complete idiot, I don't want to dictate the entire story.

When I asked for space, she gave it to me. She didn't talk to me for over a month. Somewhere it helped me understand what's going on in my mind much better, but if I ever ask for space from someone, I really want you to come down to me. The group of 4 shattered, just because I asked for space from her, my chataka pataka friend and the other one gave it to me too, and stopped talking to me, because I asked for space from her, made me wonder if they were ever friends with me? Then instead of them saving me from the so-called "kuva", they decided to let me drown and learn the lessons all by myself. Thank you so much. I left the group of 4, none of them asked me or texted me, why. They gave me the space I never asked for, and in the end I had to keep my ego aside and ask them to add me back, I agree, leaving the group might be a big move for them, but I guess my love language has always been blocking, leaving, unfollowing but for not more than a day.

There were other breakdowns, smaller and larger. The bench-partner misunderstanding — a conversation meant to protect, misreported and magnified — became a wedge I tried and failed to pry open. In November 2024 I stopped trying to repair that particular bond. I remember the exact tiredness of that day: the resignation felt like a clean cut, and yet I grieved for the friend-version I'd adored. I carried the memory of her returning from her hometown just to be at my surprise party; I carried the grief of being the person she believed the rumor about. The math of friendships is painful: sometimes your investment in someone doesn't reciprocate; sometimes loyalty is owed to the loudest person in the room.

Worse things happened. Technology turned cruel: AI-generated nudes and doctored images circulated like weapons meant to humiliate. I saw myself reduced to a set of pixels other people could weaponize. My father fought for me; my home trembled under the shock. I had panic attacks for the first time — blackouts of air and sense — and for a while I was convinced the world had no room for me. College administrators whispered that constant talking and laughing could get me removed. The suffocating campus tried to erase the person I'd been: loud, messy, alive. People I had trusted choose convenience over clarity. I felt abandoned at my worst moment.

And yet: the pillars. Two girls from school who listened to the same rant five times and never said "we're tired of you". A college classmate who stayed with me in the washroom when the world felt too heavy to stand in. My tuition friend — the one who once thought I stole her pouch and made me call my mother — who became a constant when the rest dissolved into noise. The childhood friend from the Cambridge section who still writes letters on my birthdays. The nani-house mirror-friend who reads before breakfast and yells with the same volume as I do — she became a mirror and a megaphone. And my brother: loud, immature, ridiculous, and the most faithful presence, shouting pride for me in rooms where no one else did. The school friend of mine from the college, who held onto me even after numerous fights, the girl I go to my college with, my other family friend. These people held onto me in ways I hadn't known I needed. And maybe that's why, even in the worst storms, I survived. Because I was never really alone.

But through all of this — the rumors, the screenshots, the betrayals, the suffocating college rules — my family was my anchor. I don't say this lightly. I have been the kind of daughter who has snapped at her mother, screamed at her brother, ignored her dadi, taken her dad for granted, yet they've never stopped showing up for me. Not once.

My dad — the man who doesn't sit with me much, who has never been the "let's talk for hours" father, was always the first to stand behind me when I needed him. He's the one who spends money on me without a second thought, who, when I ask for something, just makes it happen. And now, as I step into college, I see him slowly changing — sitting around me, giving me the time he never used to, trying in his own quiet way to let me know that I'm his girl. That means everything.

My mom — she is the fire and thunder and has the biggest, softest heart. She never once told me, "You have to go to IIT". I was the one who projected that dream onto her, the one who announced it as if it was hers. And when I shattered it, when I told her I didn't want JEE, she didn't shatter me back. She taunted, yes — but that's her language of love. She supported me even when I was dismantling the version of me she thought I wanted to be. She has been my 1am tea companion, my midnight soup deliverer, the person who wakes up at ungodly hours to check if I'm studying, to make sure I eat, to fight with me and still be proud of me. I can never repay her. But I want to. I want to make her dreams come true — to take her around the world, to show her the countries she's only seen on postcards.

My dada, my dadi — the kind of love that doesn't need performance. My dada was my safe place, my biggest cheerleader, and losing him tore a piece of me I'll never get back. My dadi still carries me with prayers and pride. My cousins — chaos and comfort in equal measure. My sisters — the ones I've played, fought, and grown with. My bhuas — one teaching me how to manifest, one reminding me of my potential, one I pray won't judge me too harshly when she reads this book.

It's them. Always them. Even in the years I thought I was left behind by friends, even in the classrooms where people whispered, even in the rumors that crushed me, it was my family that refused to let me go. They are my net, my proof that unconditional love exists in this world.

And maybe that's why, even in the worst storms, I survived. Because I was never really alone.

I still fight with my family. God, I fight with them a lot. My mother and I can go from screaming at each other to sitting side by side in silence in the span of an hour. My dad doesn't always get me, and I don't always get him. My brother and I can clash like anything. But the truth is, I'll always have great relations with them, no matter what. Because under all the fights, all the stubbornness, all the slammed doors and rolled eyes, there's love so deep that it doesn't crack.

I'll always be the daughter who finds peace both far and at home. Far — when I'm out chasing the world, sitting in a café alone, or dreaming of cities I haven't seen yet. And at home — in my mother's midnight tea, in my dad's quiet presence, in the chaos of cousins, in the comfort of knowing I'll never run out of love here.

The year taught me a harsh curriculum: people are not always obliged to stay; you cannot manufacture trust by pleading. I learned the difference between toxic self-center and healthy self-preservation. I learned you can be both wildly social and outrageously able to sit with your own company. I learned to go get waffles by myself, wander into a café without a date, accept a solo table and read, laugh, and pay my bill without feeling incomplete. I learned that being left behind doesn't equal being unloved — sometimes it's the only way to become unleashed. The girl who didn't step even in her colony without a company can now go around all by herself.

There were tiny rebellions that felt huge in their moment: a surprise visit that made me cry into my friend's jacket, video calls till four in the morning that ended in laughter so real it almost healed, a Singles Day speech I gave on Valentine's because we celebrated the stubbornness of choosing yourself. There was the ridiculous "cycle-wala" episode where we were accused of following someone we hadn't — pathetic at the time, but in hindsight a comic illustration of how far we'd go to feel seen. There were Navratri nights and Friendship Day plans that, even when they crumbled, left imprints — photos, reels, the taste of matcha spilled on a chilly terrace after midnight.

I stopped trying to be the entertainer of everyone's life. The people who were friends only because I filled a role — the loud centerpiece, the person who could make things happen — evaporated when I demanded reciprocity. Some of them didn't even ask me back into the group; they assumed I'd return on cue. That hollowed me out. Since January 1, 2025, everything felt sharper: losses accumulated, the dreams I'd been carrying — IIT, the polished "I'm going to succeed" narratives — wilted under a different kind of clarity. I visited a career counselor, finally spoke out that I didn't want JEE anymore, that I wanted to chase communications, management, AI — things that fit how I wanted to move through the world. Telling my mother felt like carving a soft place into the future; she taunted, she worried, but she loved me anyway. She was, and still is, my harbor.

I am not the same girl who needed to wake up every morning with a hundred people's approval. I am not the girl who couldn't bear being alone in a café. Now I can sit across from myself and call it company. I have scars and stitches: the bench-partner's silence, the mutual's coldness, the sting of seeing three people scroll and tag while I stand outside their laughter. I have gratitude too — for the friends who brought me waffles to my house, for surprise reunions that left me crying and laughing at once, for the two girls who never once demanded for me to be different to be loved.

I still love the guy who gave me his sweatshirt so that I didn't get caught by my college's peon, people who were spontaneous with me, vulnerable with me, took millions of pictures, made reels, bought coffee below my house, the girl who was in the washroom with me for an hour during the outrage, Shredding trauma, fights, love. The one who hugged me tight sitting on my lap when I burst out open.

I still hope for reconciliations. I still dream we'll go to concerts together someday, live in the same building, survive a skydiving trip and call it a ritual. Lowkey I still want to be a part of that group of four, and talk with them for the rest of the night, make them be friends with my college friends, show them around if I am somewhere new, have that silly packet of chatpataka and let them pay for it. But this time it's about who should approach first, them or me. I hold that hope differently now: not as an expectation but as a wish that can be granted or denied by time. Either way, I've learned to walk without waiting for handholds.

This chapter — these years — taught me resilience, self-possession, and the awful necessity of choosing yourself when the people around you choose differently. Left behind at eleven doesn't mean left without a future. It means you were given space to rebuild, to understand who stays when the dust settles, and who simply carried you for a season. From just being rusticated, to accepting my flaws and loving them, from being unfriended and distanced by people I'd put before the love of my life, to somewhere daydreaming about really finding the right ones. From being ungrateful and cursing my life, to seeing how privileged I am that I can study, and eat and have an amazing teen life. Chasing storms, thundering life, I can finally take a solo trip, thinking it's not so uncool.

And somewhere under all of this: grief. I lost my chote dada, the one who used to call me at my slightest inconvenience, never backing off to be proud about having such a daughter. He's still praising me from the sky above and beyond, giving me the strength and power to not uphold things but to be courageous enough to accept my biggest fears and dive in them till I reach the shore.

I lost other things too — illusions, friendships, a complacent faith that tomorrow would mirror yesterday. Those losses are heavy. They are real. But they are the kind of losses that, in time, teach you how to hold someone else when their world breaks. But these are nothing compared to my dada.

I want them back in the best-case story of my life. I want our old playlist and our terrible inside jokes and the five-a.m. terrace Maggi runs. I want the reunion scenes and the shared weddings and the concerts where we all dance like there is no hurt between us. But even if the grand reconciliations never arrive (which I do believe will arrive), I am learning how to be whole amid absence. I can be a home for myself. And that — messy, lonely, terrifying, triumphant — is something worth surviving for.

I still believe that best friend's love, attach to things, places, that I will meet someone as loud as me, but it's just that I've always wanted them to stick around me from the very start of my life, I guess you don't always get what you want, and that's fine because I have gotten more than I asked for, people out there deserve this, but someone chose me to have this. I might have done something right. Even friendships born from desperation taught me resilience. Being left behind didn't mean I was alone. Isolation didn't mean hopelessness. You find your people. You find your space. You find your love. Even alone. Even in the strangest corner. Even all by yourself.

Everything I never planned.

My life back then, I hate it as hell.
I was ecstatic which raised my expectations-
So it drowned me now and then.
The hues of the rain now correspond to black sky,
Back then, they were the rainbows who brightened my prettiest lies.

I used to laugh in the storms, thinking it loved me back,
But, the thunder only echoed the hope I lacked.
I mistook chaos for adventure and silence for grace,
And wondered why I couldn't keep up with the race.

But somewhere between crying and clearing the air,
I learned that peace wasn't loud- it was just fair.
Expectations drowned me, yes- but also made space,
For surprises I never imagined would take their place.

I still dance in the rain just with better shoes,
And when the sky turns black,I smile at the hues.
Turns out the prettiest lies lead to honest truths,
And the best kind of joy? - is that kind of soothes.

So now, I'm not bitter,
Just better at the art,
Of laughing through lighting,
And softening my heart.

Chapter 10

The Unfinished Diary

The diary isn't totally over, it's just paused. The teenage cares, heartbreaks, and wild nights out aren't done shaping me. It makes the book feel open-ended, like life itself.

Here's the truth I never wrote in the earlier pages: the things people would whisper about me if they knew. Yes, I've dated. More than once. Yes, I've sneaked out of the house at 1 a.m., barefoot, phone on silent, heart racing, pretending I was asleep under my blanket. Yes, I've kissed when my age was something I should've considered, I was offered 2000 to kiss a guy when I was in grade 8, of course I slapped him. Yes, I've texted people I had no business texting. Yes, I've stalked crushes online until 3 a.m., imagining conversations that never happened.

I've bunked lectures not just to rest but to sit with people once I called home, scream songs into the air, and eat chips for breakfast. I've lied to my parents so I could feel free for just one night. I've scrolled through chats I should've deleted long ago, reread messages until they burned, and then deleted them just to cry about losing them.

I've been jealous of my own friends, hated them and loved them at the same time. I've written letters I never sent, made playlists for people who'll never listen to it, prayed for ex-crushes to miss me. I've said "I'm fine" even when I was shaking inside. I've made my own rumors worse by feeding them with silence.

And yes, I've wanted revenge. I've wanted to prove people wrong so badly it kept me awake more than heartbreak ever could. I've imagined my "comeback moment" like it was a movie scene, every time.

But none of these secrets scare me anymore. They're just part of being seventeen—messy, reckless, impulsive, stupid, thrilling. The kind of things that make you laugh years later and say, God, I was wild.

So this diary? It's not ending. It's just pausing, waiting for me to come back with even crazier confessions, even bigger storms, even bolder love. Because I know myself—I'm not done yet.

This isn't closure. This is just the cliffhanger.

Acknowledgement

This book isn't just mine. It belongs to everyone who ever held me, scolded me, laughed with me, cried with me, left me, loved me, betrayed me, taught me, and even to the strangers who probably don't even remember my name.

First, always, my mom — the midnight tea-maker, the angry bird who still shows up at 1 a.m. just to check if I'm breathing through my exam notes. And my dad, who didn't always sit beside me but never failed to show up in the ways only he could — the man who believed in me quietly, who spent on me when I didn't even know how to ask, and who is now, as I move into college, finally sitting with me, talking to me, as if time slowed down just for us. To my dada, who brought me chocolates, and my dadi, who made sure I ate when I didn't want to. To my chacha, my chachi, my nana, my nani, and all my bhuvas who taught me everything from manifesting dreams to surviving heartbreaks. To my cousins and my younger siblings who kept me grounded in the loudest, most chaotic ways — you'll never know how much you've saved me. And my mama, especially my mama, who let me rant about my mom without ever betraying me — my family's secret-keeper, my quietest friend.

To my teachers, my tutors, my bus partner who turned into my best friend, my bench partner who shared every silly note and every serious silence, the girl who called me endlessly, the girl from Cambridge, the girl from tuition, the one who betrayed me, the one who hugged me, the one who hated me, the one who stayed anyway. To the guy who gave me his sweatshirt, to the crush who probably doesn't even know he's this book's ghost character, to his friends, to my exes — even the Gurgaon boy, even the U.S. boy. To my friends who danced with me, laughed with me, celebrated Singles Day with me, or simply stood near me when I was too angry to speak. To the college girls who still sit with me, my E5 classmates, my teammates, my management seniors, my SGI people, my collage crowd. To my school that shaped me, my principal, my class teachers, my dance teachers. To everyone who pushed me down and everyone who lifted me up — you're all here, stitched between my words.

And then, to the worlds that raised me when reality was too much. To Disney Channel — the kingdom that made childhood glitter. To Wizards of Waverly Place, Hannah Montana, The Suite Life of Zack and Cody, Good Luck Charlie, and Shake It Up — you gave me my laughter, my fashion phases, my dance moves in front of the mirror. To Sabrina Carpenter, Olivia Rodrigo, Taylor Swift — you were my heartbreak translators, the girls who put my teenage chaos into lyrics before I had the courage to write them myself. To Victoria Justice and Victorious, Jessie, and even Shinchan — for keeping me both silly and sane. To Harry Potter — the spells I still wish were real, the midnight rereads that made me braver. To Death Note and every anime that kept me awake at 3 a.m. To Love Nikki, the game that let me dress up the way reality wouldn't allow me. To every YouTuber — Ashish Chanchlani, CarryMinati, MostlySane, Bhuvan Bam — you were my comedy, my rebellion, my escape during online classes I pretended to attend.

And of course, to music itself — the playlists that made me cry when I needed to, that made me dance in my room when no one was watching. Olivia, Taylor, Sabrina — you three especially stitched my diary into songs. And of course, how could I forget my colony friends—the ones who turned empty lanes into playgrounds, who danced with me in the rain, cycled with me till our legs gave up, played badminton in the early mornings, and made lockdown feel less like a cage and more like a festival. To my football teammates and even the opponents who challenged me, who made me push myself harder, scream louder, and play braver—you'll always be a part of my fire. To my coaches, who believed in me not just when I was winning but also when I was breaking, when I was learning, when I was falling apart—you kept me standing tall. To the social media worlds—Instagram, YouTube, TikTok, all those wild online communities where I found laughter, comfort, connection, and sometimes even heartbreak—you've been as real as any classroom. And above all, to God—for being my quiet witness, my secret listener, the one who knew every single thing even when I didn't have the words.

And thank you to the things that shaped me as much as people did — Harry Potter marathons, Instagram scrolls, late night YouTube, random series that distracted me when I was falling apart, Taylor, Olivia and Sabrina and all the guys who invented music. Thank you, God, for somehow holding me through storms I didn't think I'd survive.

This isn't a neat thank-you list, because my life was never neat. But if you're reading this and we've ever crossed paths, please know: a part of you is hidden somewhere in these pages.

The Last Folded Page

Every diary has that one folded page — the one you don't write on, but you know it's there, waiting. This book is mine. And now, maybe, it's yours too.

I've spilled my stories, my heartbreaks, my rebellions, my glitter and my shadows. But the beauty of diaries is that they never really end — they echo in the lives of the people who read them.

So if you're holding this, I hope you remember that your chaos is also worth writing. Your heartbreaks deserve poetry. Your victories deserve ink. And your unfinished parts — they're not flaws, they're the proof that you're still alive, still growing, still becoming.

This Page Belongs to You

This diary isn't just mine anymore — it's yours too. This page is for you to spill your own secrets, scribble your own heartbreaks, and write the little joys you'll never forget. Connect with me by connecting with yourself here. Write what you'd never say out loud, write the things you'd want someone to read years later, or just doodle your heart out. This is your space.

Your turn,

@the.teenagediary